D0064907

EDEN'S GARDEN

EDEN'S GARDEN

•

Jane McBride Choate

AVALON BOOKS
NEW YORK

Published by Avalon Books,
an imprint of Thomas Bouregy & Co., Inc.
160 Madison Avenue, New York, NY 10016

Library of Congress Cataloging-in-Publication Data

Choate, Jane McBride.
   Eden's garden / Jane McBride Choate.
      p. cm.
   ISBN 978-0-8034-7793-3 (hardcover : acid-free paper)
1. Women pediatricians—Fiction.   2. Community gardens—
Fiction.   I. Title.
   PS3553.H575E34 2010
   813'.54—dc22

                                                    2010018143

PRINTED IN THE UNITED STATES OF AMERICA
ON ACID-FREE PAPER
BY HADDON CRAFTSMEN, BLOOMSBURG, PENNSYLVANIA

To my Red Hat sisters everywhere.
Remember: well-behaved women rarely make history.

My sincere thanks to all the editors and staff at Avalon, who make writing a joy.

Chapter One

Adam Forsythe wore a smile that made his face hurt. He propped himself against a wall of the opulent ballroom of the country club and tried to think of a reason not to strangle himself with the black tie that felt like a noose around his neck . . . and wondered why he was taking up space in the crowded room.

He supposed the silk draperies and lush flowers, marble floors and crystal chandeliers lent some class to what was essentially high-class begging.

For himself, he'd rather write a check and spend the evening at home with a good book. He cared little about attending such affairs, cared less about being seen at them. The glad-handing, backslapping, and air-kissing were not his style and never would be.

There were too many people who believed they had claim on his time and too few who had anything to say. He'd already made his plan. One hour. When it was up, he was out of there.

When he'd been a cop, he'd had no need to attend

high-class shindigs. As an assistant district attorney, he'd been required to attend a select number. Now that he was running for a city council slot, he was expected to make an appearance.

Or so said his campaign manager.

Social duties were just that. Duties. And didn't that say it all?

They were all there—the A-list of Eagleton society. The movers and the shakers, the powerful and the elite. Members of the press were discreetly stalking the more well-known of the guests, documenting the dresses, the jewels, the hair, who was dancing with whom, and, more important, who had snubbed whom.

He felt a scowl crawl cross his face and made an effort to wipe it away. Resigned that he had another fifty-one minutes and twenty-two seconds left of his self-imposed sentence, he settled back to do what he did best. Dissecting, observing.

He didn't mind looking at people when they were all sleek and slick and trying to look better than the people they were talking to. It reminded him of watching a play. As long as he could sit in the audience, he could manage for another—he checked his watch once more—forty-nine minutes.

Most of the faces were familiar. That was one of the problems with these affairs. The same people, the same music, the same food. He winced as the already loud music ratcheted up another notch. The music was too loud, the food too rich.

Adam had grown up among these people. His family was old money. The term always amused him. *Old* money, like that of the Forsythe family, was considered to be several steps above *new* money, like that of the upstarts who tried to force their way into Eagleton "society."

His mother had made it her life's work to maintain the rigid status quo, which meant keeping any newcomers out.

He'd stopped caring nearly thirteen years ago, when he'd defied his parents' wishes and joined the Eagleton police force. Along the way he'd earned a law degree.

After eight years, watching criminals he'd arrested slip through loopholes in the law had convinced him that he could change things more effectively by working inside the legal system. He'd left the force and taken the position of ADA.

He'd spent another five years working within the judicial system, growing more frustrated with every passing day. The courts couldn't keep up with the growing number of crimes, especially those committed by young offenders. It twisted his insides to see kids who hadn't yet reached eighteen being sent to prison.

For as long as he could remember, he'd wanted to make a difference, to use whatever talents he'd been given to help others. He supposed it sounded pompous, the idea that he could make a difference—worse, he feared, naive.

His years on the force had wiped most of the naivete from him. Five years as an assistant district attorney had almost completely erased any remaining traces. He'd seen the worst that one human being could do to another. And still he and others kept trying.

He knew he still bore the stamp of the cop he'd once been. Those who had spent time in a cell recognized it in him: reflexes on the alert; eyes focused, steady, flat.

Some things you didn't lose when you turned in the badge. He doubted that any of those present at tonight's affair knew he had already categorized them, filed away descriptions ready to bring out again should the need arise.

He'd made the mistake of falling into cop-speak at another such gathering. A frown and shake of the head from Russ Delroy, his campaign manager, had shut Adam up.

"That's not the way to win votes," Russ had warned him.

It bothered him—it bothered him a lot—that he had to guard his tongue, to tone down what he wanted to say, what needed to be said.

But he was learning. There was, Russ had told him, a time and a place to talk plainly, and a time and a place to make nice.

Tonight's function was the latter. School his tongue and keep his smile in place.

With that in mind, he looked for a way to get through the evening without succumbing to the mind-numbing boredom he felt setting in.

He let his eyes roam around the room, his gaze zeroing in on a woman, the shiny length of her red hair a vivid contrast to the pale blond and tidy brunet of the other women present. Neither did she wear the expected designer gown. Instead, her petal pink dress looked like a fresh flower among the overdone jewel tones of hothouse blooms. Her lips curled a bit at the corners, as though she were trying to suppress a smile.

He didn't recognize her as one of the regulars at such affairs. She might be a member of the country-club set who were routinely invited to such posh affairs, but instinct told him she wasn't. Not media either, since she didn't wear the requisite ID badge. In a room full of beautiful women, she seemed to stand alone with her gaze full of indulgent humor.

An older lady—Adam placed her as the mother of the mayor—put a hand on the woman's arm and said something. The woman smiled and nodded. Then she raised her head and caught him staring at her. She didn't look away.

Other than the one exchange with the mayor's mother, she didn't make a move to join the conversations buzzing around her. The humor in her eyes had him wondering what she found so amusing.

Clearly, she was entertained. *By what?* he wondered. The affair, like others of its kind, was so dry as to suck the life from everyone present.

Unable to stop himself, he headed in her direction. With a practiced smile, a vague gesture, he managed to sidestep those who tried to detain him.

He reached his goal and stopped. "You look like you've got the secret."

She tilted her head. "What secret would that be?"

"Getting through the night without losing your mind."

A full smile bloomed on her heart-shaped face. "Maybe I do."

"Care to share it?"

"Only if you'll share some of that with me." She glanced at his full plate.

Obligingly, he held out the plate. She helped herself to a sliver of smoked salmon. "Thanks. I couldn't brave the buffet table."

He grinned, appreciating her. The delicacy-laden table was guarded by a gauntlet of society matrons, each devoted to snaring anyone within reach and pumping them for their credentials.

Adam knew the drill. Where were you born? What was your mother's maiden name? How did you rate receiving an invitation? Then, if you passed muster, you were deemed acceptable and favored with a smile.

"Smart lady."

She dipped her head in acknowledgment.

A cop, he was trained to notice physical details. Like the tiny birthmark on her collarbone. And the way her hair held a hundred different shades, ranging from the palest gold to the richest auburn.

"Pay up."

"Ah. The secret." She lowered her voice and gave a conspiratorial smile. "I imagine everyone here in their underwear."

The absurdity of the statement caught him unaware. Then he laughed heartily, earning curious stares from those nearby.

He stuck out his hand. "Adam Forsythe."

She put her hand in his. "Eden Hathaway. And I know who you are. You're part of the reason I'm here tonight." She paused. "I need your help."

He suppressed a groan and a twinge of disappointment. *Here it comes.* Since he'd announced that he was running for the city council, people had been crawling out of the woodwork, wanting things from him. The election was weeks away, but the requests kept coming.

"What can I do for you, Ms. Hathaway?" he asked, not bothering to hide the resignation in his voice.

"It's Dr. Hathaway, and it's about tonight's benefit."

"What about it?"

"We're about halfway to our goal, and—"

He held up a hand. "Just a minute. Who's 'we'?"

"Grow a Garden, Grow a Child."

"You're a volunteer?"

"You could say that. I'm one of the founders."

That explained a lot. "If you'll come by my office tomorrow, I'll be happy to write a check."

"Thanks, but that's not what I want."

Since when did a representative from a charity turn down money? His interest piqued, he asked, "What do you want?"

"I want you to be a spokesperson for our group." Her words came out in a rush, as if the feeling behind them couldn't be contained a moment longer. "If someone like you speaks out, people will listen."

Adam thought the woman was incredibly naive if she thought he, alone, could do anything. Hadn't he just applied the same label to himself for believing he could do that very thing? "You really think one person's going to make a difference?"

"One person, one voice, can always make a difference." She twisted her hands. "You're a public figure, Mr. Forsythe—and about to become even better known. If you'll lend your support to our cause, others will too. If people know and understand just what the need is, they'll be more willing to support the community garden we want to start. We need endorsement from a public figure." She paused, looking straight at him, her dark blue eyes challenging him to accept.

"Look, Ms. Hathaway, I have at least a dozen requests

each day to support one cause or another. What makes yours so special?"

"Because every child deserves to have enough food. A community garden will help. Picture it: people growing their own food, feeding their children freshly picked vegetables and fruit. The possibilities are endless. Families working together, creating something." She shot a withering look at him. "Obviously, that means nothing to someone like you, but it does to me."

"What do you mean, 'someone like me'?"

"Adam Forsythe. Son of Matthew and Kitty Forsythe. The best prep school. The best college. The best of everything. Ex-cop. Assistant district attorney. Candidate for city council."

"So you know my background. So does everyone else who's opened a newspaper."

"Have you ever been hungry, Mr. Forsythe? So hungry that the emptiness presses against your stomach until you stop feeling it?"

"No, but—"

"I didn't think so. I'm sorry I wasted your time." She walked away without a backward glance.

It nettled him. She had told him in no uncertain terms that she found him lacking. Her bluntness had caught him by surprise, and, oddly, his respect for her went up another notch.

Adam stared after her, aware that he'd been evaluated and found wanting. She'd neatly tagged him as rich, pampered, and spoiled. It wasn't the first time such labels had been attached to his name, and it wouldn't be the last. He'd decided a long time ago he wouldn't let it bother him.

Wasn't that an irony? To discover that he found this woman, a woman who had no use for him, more intriguing than any woman he'd met in months. Perhaps years.

What did that say about him?

Adam didn't try to analyze why finding out more about Eden Hathaway was so important. But he intended to do so.

The memory of the cool contempt in her eyes stayed with him for the rest of the evening.

At home, Eden blew out a frustrated breath, then swallowed hard.

She had done her homework on Adam Forsythe. Expoliceman turned attorney turned politician. That wasn't what had made her seek him out. The headlines aside, he had a reputation for caring about the community, about people.

When she had heard him speak at a rally about helping the city's poor, she thought she'd found someone who believed as she did.

Affairs like tonight's weren't a usual part of her routine. Now that she'd experienced the benefit for her pet causes she understood why so many of those present wore twin expressions of boredom and resentment.

When she'd read Adam Forsythe's name on tonight's guest list, she'd seized upon it as an opportunity to enlist his support for the community garden her group wanted to start.

But, as always, when she felt passionately about something, she'd plunged in without thinking the matter through. She didn't blame him—entirely—for refusing her request.

She'd led with her heart instead of her head and, in doing

so, alienated the one man who might have been willing to help. She pressed away the regret but knew it would return.

A cloud of failure settled over her spirits as she acknowledged that she was also in large part to blame. She'd come on too strong, too fast. Still, that didn't excuse Forsythe's callousness in turning her down flat, she thought with a return of resentment.

Just as quickly as the anger appeared, it dissolved. Still, she couldn't help the disappointment that she'd misread the man so completely.

She'd thought Adam Forsythe was different from other wealthy men. But she'd been wrong. It wasn't the first time she'd misjudged a man.

She pushed aside those feelings and concentrated on the papers in front of her. Grow a Garden would net a huge amount from tonight's benefit. Combined with what was already in the treasury, the group would have enough to start looking for the right piece of land.

It was up to her and the others on the site committee to start scouting out locations. Once they had a piece of land, they could start working.

Grow a Garden, Grow a Child—a way to help people help themselves—had been her idea. The diseases that could be prevented with proper nutrition were endless. She'd seen firsthand what malnutrition did to young bones, young bodies, young minds. Pregnant women could give their babies a boost before they were even born.

The garden had been her brainchild. Now it was her dream.

* * *

The phone hadn't stopped ringing since Adam stepped into his office at eight the following morning. By noon, he decided he needed to have the receiver surgically removed from his ear.

He buzzed his secretary, Harriet, on the intercom. "Hold my calls."

"Until when?"

He looked at his desk, piled high with yesterday's mail, mock-ups for campaign ads, and heaven knew what else. "Until I tell you differently."

"Sure thing, boss."

Adam smiled as he switched off the intercom. Harriet had been with him from the beginning, a holdover from his first year as an ADA.

He didn't know what he'd do without her; he didn't want to find out. If he won the seat on the council, he was going to depend upon her more than ever. She knew more about the business of politics than anyone in the city, including him. She was fond of saying that what she didn't know wasn't worth knowing.

He pulled out a sample campaign brochure Russ had designed. Adam groaned as he read the text extolling his virtues and departmental record. And the picture of him in his cadet uniform—where had Russ come up with that? It had to be thirteen years old.

Adam scrawled one word across the pamphlet. *No.*

He grinned briefly. Russ would have a fit, but that couldn't be helped. Adam hadn't been altogether certain about entering the race for city council, but since he had, he was determined to run his campaign as he ran his life: no false promises, only honest, hard work.

Methodically, he worked his way through the remaining papers on his desk. When he pushed back his chair a couple of hours later, he let out a sigh of satisfaction.

Idly, he picked up the phone book and flipped through it until he came to the *H*'s. He ran his finger down the list of names until he found the one he was looking for. *Hathaway, E.*

The woman's accusations had bothered him more than he cared to admit, primarily because he feared they might be true. He hadn't experienced hunger. Ever. A guilty twinge nagged at his conscience. Perhaps he'd been too quick to dismiss her and her request.

Before he could talk himself out of it, he punched in her number. "Dr. Hathaway? It's Adam Forsythe. I wanted to apologize for last night. I wonder if you'd have lunch with me today."

Adam was smiling as he recradled the phone a few minutes later. Eden Hathaway had class, he decided. He hadn't expected and certainly didn't deserve her graciousness in accepting his apology.

He found himself looking forward to a lunch date for the first time in a very long while.

He was nearly late when he entered the restaurant, but a glance around confirmed that Eden wasn't there yet either. A waiter showed him to a table.

Eden arrived moments later. "Am I late?" she asked, her voice a trifle breathless.

"No." He stood and pulled out a chair for her.

Her eyes warmed by several degrees, and her lips tipped up in a smile. "Good. Because I'm hungry."

He felt himself responding to the smile, to her. Her frankness disarmed him, as did the clear blue eyes gazing back at him.

While she studied the menu, he let his gaze linger on her red hair, framing her face with soft curls. Her lips were full and bare of lipstick.

Soft color suddenly smudged her cheeks. "You're staring at me," she said.

Adam smiled, enchanted. When was the last time he'd seen a woman blush? "Sorry. I didn't mean to embarrass you."

A waiter appeared.

The color heightened in her cheeks. "I . . . you . . . shall we order?"

After they'd placed their orders, Adam asked, "How did a doctor become involved with last night's charity?"

"I'm a pediatrician. I've seen too many children develop diseases they shouldn't get simply because they didn't have the proper nutrition. So I took a sabbatical from my job and decided to address the root of the problem. I couldn't keep practicing medicine when it wasn't medicine that needed changing. It was the way we as a society neglect our children, our poor."

He noticed her use of words. *Our children.* "You're amazing."

"No. I'm just someone who wants to help kids." She paused. "I have to admit I wasn't sold on the idea of the benefit at first. It seemed like a waste of resources. But the group I work with—Grow a Garden, Grow a Child—decided it would be a great moneymaker. And it was." She grinned. "Thanks to you and all the others who paid the price of admission."

Her smile invited him to join her. Five hundred dollars a plate wasn't unusual for such events.

"Tell me about your group," he said.

She studied him frankly.

Adam was surprised to find himself fighting the urge to squirm under her scrutiny. Not many people had that effect on him. Of course, not many people looked him straight in the eye with the unblinking gaze Eden was subjecting him to now.

"Just remember," she warned. "You asked."

He sat back, prepared to listen.

She leaned forward, her elbows propped on the table, chin resting on her clasped hands. "Our goal is to keep our local children from ever going hungry. The money from last night and other fund-raisers will go to start a community garden."

"What's a community garden?"

"Just what the name says. People growing healthy food for themselves and their families. Once we find the right site, we can start right in and be planting fruits and vegetables this coming spring."

He listened as she described the efforts that would go into preparing the ground, planting, cultivating, and then harvesting.

"That's the best part, the harvesting. Can't you see it?" she asked, her eyes filled with excitement. "Parents and children working alongside one another. Growing their own food, eating well, and knowing they did something worthwhile together. Some of these children have never known the satisfaction of planting a seed, then seeing it grow into something beautiful."

While she talked, Adam watched her. She wasn't beautiful, not in the accepted sense of perfect features, but her eyes held compassion and a warmth that drew him even as he told himself he should stay away.

After talking for nearly twenty minutes, she flushed. "I'm sorry. Once I get started, I can't seem to stop."

"Don't apologize. I like listening to you." He meant it.

Eden looked uncertain. Her slender throat moved up and down as she swallowed a few bites of her salad. He smiled encouragingly, and soon the words were tumbling out again. Her face grew animated as she used her fork to emphasize a point.

"There's nothing as delicious as a just-picked tomato," she said. "Or corn harvested when it's as sweet as candy. I want that for our children. If every child, every expectant mother, had the right food, it would solve so many problems."

Adam asked questions, wanting to keep her talking. She rewarded him with another one of those smiles that threatened to turn him inside out. Her voice, low and musical, worked its own magic, and he let it spread its warmth over him. He hadn't realized how edgy he'd been lately until he felt the tension melt away under the soft cadence of her voice.

When their meals arrived, they were still talking, Adam still trying to comprehend how so many people could go hungry in the richest country on the earth and Eden challenging his preconceived ideas. He watched as a range of emotions passed over her face with every word she spoke.

Eagleton was not a very big city, but he knew it had its problems. All communities did. Still, he hadn't realized the extent that actual malnutrition plagued his hometown.

He said as much to Eden—and was surprised by her smile.

"You're starting to understand," she said.

He studied her hands. They were small, like the woman herself. They were also capable looking, the skin slightly roughened, evidence of hard work.

It intrigued him. *She* intrigued him.

He'd done his own homework. It hadn't been hard to find out the who and the what of Dr. Eden Hathaway. She had graduated second in her class, then turned down offers from large teaching hospitals all over the country to work at the county hospital.

The small facility couldn't afford the salaries of the bigger ones. He reflected on what she'd already given up to live and work here. And now she'd even taken a sabbatical to tackle the problems of Eagleton's poor?

"What about your personal life?" he asked. "You do have a personal life, don't you?"

"Of course."

"Tell me about it."

"I volunteer at the homeless shelter, free clinic, and community food pantry. When I'm not at the shelter or teaching classes at the clinic on prenatal and childhood nutrition, I'm trying to find a site for Grow a Garden. If we find the right place, we can start wading through all the paperwork and be ready to plant in the spring."

"Did you hear what you just told me?" He didn't wait for her answer. "You volunteer at the shelter and food pantry and free clinic, teach classes, and work to get a community garden started. What do you do for *you,* for Eden the woman?"

"It's you who isn't hearing. I do all those things for me too. I love what I do." She'd spoken only the truth, but a niggle of doubt assailed her. Did she do those things because she truly enjoyed them, or were they also a way to fill the empty hours, hours she'd longed to fill with raising her own family? She pushed away the thought. Her hours weren't empty—far from it. They were filled to capacity.

"Hey, I didn't mean to upset you."

"You didn't."

The dishes were cleared, the bill presented, and still they continued to talk. This time it was he who was doing the talking.

Eden had a way of listening that made him hear the meaning behind his own words. She was that rare creature—someone who could listen with her whole self.

"You care about people," he said. "That's rare today."

"Not really."

"You're so naive, you don't even realize how special that makes you."

"I stopped being naive when I saw what malnutrition does to a two-year-old. There's so much need, even here in Eagleton, I decided I had to help. By the time parents bring their children to me, it's often too late. So I started looking around me with my heart instead of just my eyes. Try it, and you might see more than you ever imagined."

He looked at her and saw the commitment, the compassion, that sparked her eyes. *No. She'd never be able to sit back and simply wait for others to help. She'd be leading the crusade.* He liked that about her. He liked *her.*

"How old are you?" he asked.

"Twenty-nine."

"You must have started practicing right out of medical school."

"I always knew I wanted to be a doctor. Once upon a time I pictured myself as one of the world's great researchers, curing every disease known to man." A faint smile rested on her lips. "Instead, I ended up here in California."

"Do you regret it?"

She looked thoughtful. "No. Working with children, for children, is what I want to do. This is where I want to be."

He paused, searching for the right words with which to apologize. The understanding in her eyes convinced him he didn't need fancy words; he only needed to say what was in his heart. "I'm sorry. You must have thought I was a real jerk, especially when I tried to pawn you off by offering to write you a check."

She shook her head. "I thought you were someone who cared but didn't understand."

"And now?"

"I think you're beginning to realize that simply throwing a little money at the problem but then turning away won't solve it."

He gave a sheepish smile. "You've got yourself a convert. Just tell me what you want me to do."

"Start talking up hunger in our community and how to fight it. Get the city council's attention. Tell your friends, your colleagues, your golf buddies—anyone who will listen. Then maybe we'll get the support we need to get our garden going."

"Done. Now it's my turn to ask a favor."

"Name it."

"Have dinner with me Friday night," he said.

She laughed. "You don't mean that."

"Yes, I do."

She shook her head. "After this lunch, you still want to risk having dinner with a do-good-ing doctor?"

A laugh escaped him. "You missed your calling. You should have been a mind reader."

"I've found my calling."

That sobered him. "I'm sorry. I didn't mean to belittle what you do."

Her fingers lightly touched his arm. "I know."

"I want to see you again. Have dinner with me. Please."

"No." She smiled to soften the refusal. "It's my turn to treat. If you come to my house, I'll cook dinner for you."

"A home-cooked meal?" The idea was more appealing than he believed possible.

"Uh-huh."

"I didn't think women cooked anymore."

"This one does. I have to if I want to eat. California county docs don't rate big salaries."

"I know. May I bring something? Wine? Dessert?"

"Dessert would be great."

"It's a date."

"A date?" She looked as though she were testing the idea. "I guess it is."

He had asked her out to lunch to apologize—and to prove to himself that she wasn't his type of woman. But his plan had backfired. This time together had made him want to spend more time with her, to get to know her better.

His lips tightened in irritation. At himself. He wasn't a green boy to fall to pieces over a pair of pretty eyes and a soft mouth. There was something about her, though, something that defied the ruthless logic he applied to the rest of his life, something he was powerless to resist.

Perhaps it was the sweet curve of her lips whenever she smiled.

No, she wasn't his usual kind of date. She didn't hang on his every word, looking up at him with simpering eyes. She had a brain, which she wasn't afraid to use, and she gave as good as she got—and then some. She stood up to him, challenged his preconceived notions of why things were the way they were, and then smiled at him so sweetly that he forgot everything but the longing to taste those sweetly curving lips.

When Eden excused herself to go to the ladies' room, Adam tried to convince himself he'd imagined the soft appeal of her smile. He stood when she returned, and, as her lips bowed up, he knew he'd only been lying to himself.

Chapter Two

For the next two days, Eden thought of little else but her upcoming dinner with Adam Forsythe. As she worked on a grant for continued funding for prenatal care for teenage mothers, she recalled Adam's face with its chiseled cheekbones and full lips. Leading her mother-baby nutrition group, she remembered his husky voice. As she volunteered at the free clinic, she wondered if he liked children.

In fact, Adam Forsythe was occupying far too many of her thoughts and far too much of her attention.

She resolved to push him from her mind. Easier said than done.

Especially when he called on Thursday to remind her of their date on Friday, his deep voice a calm anchor in the midst of chaos. Especially when he had a bouquet of violets delivered to her home. Especially when she didn't *want* to stop thinking about him.

She feared that Adam Forsythe was in her mind to stay. The only question was, did she want to let him into her life?

Everything that could go wrong on Friday managed to

do so. And then some. Eden's plans to prepare dinner and then get herself ready at a leisurely pace evaporated under a series of emergencies.

First, the ancient pipes in the free clinic's one and only restroom burst. Just as she was finishing cleaning up, a teenage mother with her baby daughter in a backpack showed up. Eden spent the next hour listening to the teenager cry as she explained that she and her parents had had a falling-out, and she had no food for her baby.

A call to the parents, their arrival at the clinic, and an hour of counseling followed, with the result that the girl, her infant daughter, and her parents returned home together with the promise to start talking and *listening* to one another.

After her morning in the clinic, Eden put in extra hours at her desk, trying to work up another budget proposal to keep the clinic open. The figures hadn't changed from the last time, though, and she sighed. The problem was always the same. There was never enough money for the "extras"—programs she considered essential.

That shortsighted attitude was going to cost more in the long run. Scrimping pennies only to spend dollars later on. She pushed her hair back from her face and looked at the clock.

Ten more minutes, she promised herself, and she'd call it quits. But ten minutes stretched into twenty, then another twenty. A glance at her watch an hour later sent her scrambling for her purse and papers.

Upon returning home, Eden started rolling out the crust for the chicken pot pie she planned to serve tonight, when the phone rang again.

"What now?"

It was the Connellys, a young couple with a new baby, desperate to find a substitute sitter so that they could have a long-anticipated evening for themselves. Zach and Anna Connelly had had a rough time of it lately. Zach, an engineer, had recently been laid off and was trying to support his family on odd jobs. At home with no car and no supportive relatives nearby, Anna struggled with the never-ending tasks of tending a baby.

Adam would understand, Eden told herself. It wasn't as if this were a real date. It was simply two people having dinner together—a dinner she still had to cook.

After the Connellys dropped Teddy off, Eden settled the baby down for a nap. She watched as he hiked his little bottom into the air and began sucking on his thumb. For a moment, Eden let her imagination take hold, pretending the baby was hers. She loved children, would like a dozen of her own.

After checking the time, she gave up thoughts of the long bath she'd planned and opted for a quick shower before preparing the remainder of the dinner.

The buzz of the doorbell an hour later had her hurriedly smoothing her hair. Then she opened the door and stood back in silent invitation for Adam Forsythe to enter.

He looked relaxed. Perhaps it was his choice of clothes: chinos, a cotton sweater with the sleeves pushed up, and scuffed loafers. To her eyes, he was more attractive than ever.

With subtly muscled shoulders and posture that was effortlessly upright, he exuded an understated masculinity that was all the more potent for its quiet assurance.

His eyes provided a contradiction, dark and brooding one moment, filled with humor the next. He had the look of a man who had seen too much of the worst the world had to offer but had somehow managed to keep his belief in the basic goodness of humankind.

She needed a diversion from her wayward thoughts. Teddy provided just that when he let out a wail. Eden excused herself, went to pick up the baby, quieting him with soft words, then returned to Adam.

She stifled a chuckle at the bemused look on his face as he took in the sight of her holding Teddy.

"We have an extra guest," she said, shifting the baby in her arms. "Some friends asked if I'd tend Teddy for them. They haven't had a night out since he was born, and the sitter they'd hired flaked out on them."

Eden gestured toward the overstuffed sofa. She wished she'd remembered to place a pillow over the most conspicuous stain in the upholstery. The sofa had been a gift from a patient's family when they moved to another city.

In fact, that was how she'd acquired most of her furniture—cast-offs, donations, and thrift-store finds. None of the pieces matched, of course, but most were gifts from the heart and, therefore, special.

Adam didn't notice the stain in the upholstery. He was too busy soaking up the feelings the house evoked. It was filled with the homey scents of cooking as well as the faint tang of lemon furniture polish.

A buzzer went off.

"Would you hold Teddy while I check on the vegetables?" she asked.

Adam gave the baby a cautious look. "Uh . . . sure."

Eden laughed. "He won't break. Babies are much tougher than they look."

She deposited Teddy in Adam's arms. He took the little boy gingerly, handing a bakery box to Eden as he did so. "Dessert."

As Teddy snuggled into his arms, Adam looked down at him with a feeling akin to awe. Wonderingly, he watched as the baby curled an entire fist around Adam's little finger.

Teddy cooed at him, his lips puckering into a tiny *o*. His fingers now closed around Adam's sweater, tugging it up to his mouth, where he started to suck on it.

Eden returned and gently disengaged Teddy's fingers and mouth. "I'm so sorry. He must be ready for a bottle. I'll go get one for him."

"It's all right." He looked down at his slightly soggy sweater. "I like it better this way."

She smiled at him approvingly. "You're doing fine," she said, before disappearing back into the kitchen.

Still wary, Adam held Teddy stiffly, breathing in the sweet scent of baby. An only child, he'd never been around little ones much, but the small bundle in his arms convinced him he'd been missing something. "I could get to like you, slugger." He stroked the downy head with its tuft of dark hair.

He'd faced down armed robbers, held his own with opposing counsel, and none of them intimidated him as much as the infant in his arms who stared up at him with chocolate brown eyes.

"Look, I don't know what I'm supposed to do with you, but if I do anything wrong, cry or something. Okay?"

A whimper was the only response.

"I guess you don't talk much, do you? That's all right. I'll let you in on a secret. I've never really talked to a baby before."

The whimpering grew more insistent.

Adam panicked and dredged up everything he'd ever heard about babies. "Do you . . . uh . . . do you like to be walked?"

The distressed cries stopped.

Taking that to be a "Yes," he circled the room, all the while keeping up a steady stream of nonsense.

"Maybe we should sit down for a while," he said.

A slight cough alerted him that he and Teddy were no longer alone. He looked up to find Eden smiling at him, a baby bottle in one hand. Adam hadn't blushed since he was thirteen years old, but he was blushing now. He felt the hot color flood his cheeks. How long had she been watching them?

"It's all right," Eden said. "There's nothing wrong with liking babies. Most people do."

"I've never been around babies much." A smile slid past his embarrassment. "Guess it's pretty obvious, huh?"

"Never," she denied. "I'd say you're a real pro."

"Really?"

"Really."

A suspicious warmth spread over his sweater. "Uh-oh."

"What is it?"

He held Teddy out, and he watched as Eden struggled not to laugh. A reluctant grin inched across his face. "I think I've just been christened."

"I think you're right. Give him to me, then take off your

sweater. If it's washable, I'll put it in the machine, and it'll be done before you leave."

He handed the tiny offender to Eden. A bit self-conscious, he yanked off his wet sweater.

Eden disappeared with it and Teddy and came back with a lavender terry robe. "Try this until your sweater's ready. I'm sorry I don't have anything bigger."

Adam stuck his arms through the sleeves and tied the belt around him. The sleeves barely reached his elbows; the hem of the robe hit him at mid-thigh.

Teddy squirmed in Eden's arms. "Your turn's coming," she promised.

Adam followed her into the bedroom, where she went to change Teddy's diaper. He watched as she deftly completed the maneuver. "You make it seem so easy," he said, impressed with Eden's efficiency.

"It is easy." She gave him an impish smile. "You can do the next one."

"I think I'll pass this time." With a start, he realized what he'd just said. *This time.* Would there be a next time? Spending an evening babysitting wasn't his usual idea of a good time, but then, Eden Hathaway wasn't the usual kind of woman.

He caught a glimpse of himself in the full-length mirror hanging on her bedroom door, and he groaned as he saw Eden's reflection.

She had a hand clamped over her mouth, attempting to shove down her laughter, but after a halfhearted battle, it erupted in a chuckle. With a wry look, Adam joined in.

He contrived to appear offended, and she only laughed

harder. He made a face. "I'm glad the voters can't see me now. The only vote I'd get is the sympathy one."

He was discovering that he smiled and laughed a lot when he was with Eden.

Once again he was reminded that Eden Hathaway was different from other women he'd known. He must like it, because here he was, back for more.

"You're a good sport. Not all men would take it this well." She grinned mischievously. "You look good in lavender."

"I'll remember that the next time I buy a robe."

Their laughter mingled as they looked at each other. Adam put out a hand. "Eden, I—"

Another signal from the buzzer interrupted what he'd started to say.

"Dinner's ready," she announced. She settled Teddy with his bottle, then led Adam to the table.

The chicken pot pie was a far cry from the elegant meal they'd shared two days earlier. And far more enjoyable, Adam admitted silently. No snowy linen or fine china adorned the table, only place mats, mismatched dishes, and a jelly jar holding the bouquet of violets he'd sent.

Perhaps it was the setting. Eden's tiny kitchen had its own brand of charm, wrapping itself around him, inviting him to relax. It was working, Adam realized as he helped himself to another helping of the savory pie.

"I don't usually eat this much," he said with an embarrassed smile. "After a while, restaurant food all starts to taste the same. A home-cooked meal is a real treat."

"Don't apologize. I'm glad you like it."

He remembered the cheesecake he'd brought. "Shall we have dessert?"

They moved into the living room and sat on the lumpy sofa.

He supposed the dessert was good, but he barely tasted it. He was too busy staring at Eden. She'd worn her hair loose. It tumbled around her face in a mass of unruly curls. Sooty lashes framed eyes as guileless as Teddy's.

She had a habit of pushing her hair back with both hands, an unconscious gesture that got to him every time. He wondered why until he realized that it bared her face, revealing its beauty and vulnerability.

Unable to resist, he softly touched her hair and heard her breath go out on a sigh.

As he'd done three nights earlier, he took her hand, liking the feel of it in his. Her nails were free of polish, her fingers bare of rings. Ridges of callus roughened her fingers and palms. This was a woman who wasn't afraid to work.

She didn't pull her hand away. Encouraged, he brushed his other thumb along her cheek.

"If you'd like to wait here, you could turn on the television. I'll just be a few minutes cleaning up." She abruptly stood and started to stack dishes.

"Let me help. Please," he added when he saw the uncertainty on her face.

"You don't have to."

"I know. But I want to," he said, surprised to find the words were true.

He *did* want to help. He wanted to spend time with her, even if it meant washing dishes. Besides, he had a feeling that even doing dishes would be enjoyable with Eden.

They worked side by side at the sink in companionable

silence, Eden washing the dishes and then handing them to Adam, who dried them.

A few bubbles danced through the air as she squirted more detergent into the water to wash the cookware. Some settled in her hair, glistening like diamonds against red sable. Another landed on the tip of her nose. Without thinking, Adam reached up to wipe the bubble away. His hand collided with hers.

She dropped hers and reached for a towel, dabbing her face with it.

"You should always wear bubbles." His fingers sifted through her hair. "Here." He dropped his hand to touch her nose. "And here."

"Maybe I could start a new trend."

"It'd never catch on. Any woman can wear diamonds. Only a few can wear bubbles."

"Thank you," she said softly. "I think that's the nicest compliment I've ever received."

"Then you've been seeing the wrong men."

She turned away quickly and began gathering up the washed dishes.

Adam took them from her and set them back on the counter. "I'm sorry. Did I embarrass you?"

"No . . . that is . . . I don't date all that much. I . . . don't have time."

"Then maybe it's time for a change." Gently, so very gently, he captured her face in his hands and fitted his lips to hers. She tasted sweet, incredibly sweet.

When he raised his head, he was shaken. "Don't ask me to apologize for that."

"I'm not going to. I enjoyed it."

Her honesty startled him almost as much as did the kiss. She was as guileless as a child, with her huge eyes gazing straight into his heart. He drew her to him, his hands resting at her waist.

He forgot he was wearing a terry robe several sizes too small. He forgot she was a do-good-ing doctor. He forgot everything, everything but the woman in his arms.

He didn't try to kiss her again. He was content to hold her, to feel her heart beat a rapid tattoo against his chest. Words were unnecessary, which was good, because he couldn't think of a thing to say.

A plaintive cry pierced the silence, shattering the mood.

Gently, Eden withdrew from his embrace. "I'd better check on Teddy."

Adam drew in a deep breath, not sure whether he was sorry or relieved by the interruption. Probably a little of both. What was he doing here? He had no business becoming involved with Eden Hathaway.

For the first time that evening, he let his gaze take in the mismatched furniture—from the purple shag rug to the red sofa. Odd, but somehow it all melded together. It was more of a home than that where he'd spent the first eighteen years of his life.

His mother changed the décor of the Forsythe mansion the way other people changed their hair. The only things Kitty Forsythe kept were the antiques she prized above all else.

A few minutes later, Eden reappeared. He remembered what her cheek felt like—baby soft.

As soft as her heart. The thought surprised him. He wasn't given to poetic turns of phrases. But then, Eden had him doing a lot of things he wasn't accustomed to. Things like holding a baby. Things like clearing a table and washing dishes. Things like kissing a pretty do-gooder who needed funds.

Things like wanting to kiss her again.

"I'd better go."

Did she look disappointed? He hoped so. He knew he was. But right now, he needed time away, time to put his thoughts, his feelings, into perspective. He couldn't do that when he was near Eden.

"May I call you?" he asked.

A smile chased away the disappointment—if it were disappointment—from her face. "Of course. Would you hold Teddy for a minute? I'll get your sweater."

Chagrined, Adam looked down at the lavender robe. He'd forgotten that he still wore it.

Teddy swiped a small hand at Adam's face.

"Eden's special," he whispered to the baby. "I'd like to get to know her a whole lot better."

Eden returned just then. Had she heard him?

"It's still warm from the dryer," she said as she handed the sweater to him and took Teddy.

He shrugged off the robe and slipped into the sweater. Then he brushed a finger across Eden's cheek, not trusting himself to kiss her again.

Yup. Baby soft.

Chapter Three

Pulling aside the drapes, Eden watched as Adam drove away.

Adam Forsythe was a complex man, brusque and blunt one moment, gentle and warm the next. He was also way out of her league.

He was an attractive man. It was only natural she should be drawn to him. Whatever it was, she knew she couldn't deny the stirring inside her he caused.

Maybe it was the way he looked at her, as though he saw not just the doctor but the woman inside. Maybe it was the way she felt when he took her hand or touched her hair. Maybe it was because he was by far the most intriguing man she'd met in a long time.

He was tall, but he didn't shamble. Like an athlete honed for peak performance, he was in control of his height and his body.

With his family's influence, he could have had his choice of professions. He'd chosen to join the police force. She'd read enough to know that he'd risen quickly through the ranks, making detective within a few years.

After his years on the force, he'd taken a position with the district attorney's office. Even there, he had not taken the easy path but chose to prosecute the worst crimes. Hadn't she done something similar? She'd chosen the county hospital rather than a large teaching one where she could make money and a reputation.

With a tug of shame, she realized she'd dismissed him as pampered and spoiled because of his background. Now she realized he was so much more.

Other men she'd known had been distinguished largely by their lack of distinction. She could easily put them out of her mind, if, indeed, they had ever entered it. Not so with Adam.

But she had no business thinking of him. Her life was overflowing with activities, responsibilities, and obligations as it was. She needed order, not disorder; peace, not the toe-curling excitement she knew Adam would bring to her existence.

She settled into a rocking chair, the steady motion soothing her mixed-up emotions. Teddy squirmed in her lap. Looking into the baby's eyes, Eden wondered what he thought of Adam. She couldn't help remembering how Adam had held Teddy as though he were something rare and precious.

"You like him too, don't you?"

The baby gave a contented sigh.

"I'm not surprised."

Teddy sighed again, a sound Eden took for agreement.

When Teddy's parents returned, Eden bundled him into

his snowsuit. She waved as the young couple departed amid a flurry of thank-yous and good-byes.

She lingered on the front porch, reluctant to return to the house. Under the frail illumination that filtered down from the porch light, she stared out into the night. The birds were silent now, leaving an emptiness in the air that the whisper of dying leaves in the breeze barely touched.

A pang of loneliness assailed her. She spent most of her time surrounded by people, yet she was frequently lonely. A yearning for something she couldn't define gnawed at her.

At that moment, she remembered Adam's comments about her personal life. But he was wrong. He had to be.

A chill brushed over her, and she hurried inside.

Her life was full; she didn't have time for the void he'd accused her of trying to fill. But she couldn't stop the wayward thoughts as she finished straightening up in the kitchen.

Chances were good she wouldn't be hearing from him again. After that one breath-stopping kiss, he'd beat a hasty retreat. It didn't take too much reasoning to figure out why.

He'd been disappointed. She'd known all along that Adam Forsythe was too sophisticated to be attracted to a woman like her. Still, she couldn't dispel the tiny cloud of disappointment that settled over her spirits.

He'd said he'd call—probably simply an exit line. Well, that was fine with her. She didn't need a man complicating her life. She had enough on her plate, what with raising funds for the community garden and keeping up with her other volunteer work.

No, she didn't need a man in her life right now. But

sometimes . . . sometimes . . . she wished there were someone special. Someone to share the good times with as well as the bad. Someone to chase away the loneliness. Someone to love.

She pulled her scattered thoughts back into line. Despite her best efforts, though, a shadow brushed over her heart.

When the phone shrilled, Eden picked it up on the first ring, eager to escape her thoughts.

"Doc? It's Norman Zwiebel. Hattie took a bad fall. She's at the hospital now and asking for you. I know it's late, but could you come?"

"I'll be there in ten minutes," she promised.

Hattie and Norman Zwiebel were two of Eden's favorite people. She had met the elderly couple when they volunteered to cuddle babies in the preemie unit. Despite their years, they managed to run rings around most people half their age, but a fall at eighty was serious.

Eden drove her rattletrap quickly, grateful the traffic was light at this time of night. A sliver of moon poked through the bare arms of the trees. A month earlier, it would have been kept at bay by the leaves.

She made it to the hospital in eight minutes and walked straight to the admitting desk. The receptionist directed her to the third floor, where she found Norman pacing.

Eden took a moment to steady herself. While she did so, she viewed the waiting room from the perspective of a relative or friend rather than that of a physician. She supposed all waiting rooms were the same—cold and sterile, with the requisite mass-produced paintings of mountain scenes. Uncomfortable-looking chairs lined the walls.

Overriding the standard-issue furnishings was something less tangible but more insidious. Tension. The air was thick with it, and, like a virus, it spread from one person to another, attacking anyone and everyone who walked into the room to wait.

Time stretched until every minute became a form of torture. Families huddled together, seeking to give and find comfort and hope. A young mother, two small children pressed to her side, read from storybooks, probably waiting for news on her husband.

Norman spotted her and shuffled toward her. "Thanks for coming," he said, pressing her hand between his gnarled ones.

"I'm glad you called. How is she?"

"I don't know. The surgeon took her to the OR. Her right hip's broken." His voice cracked. "What if . . . what if . . . ?" He sniffled loudly and then cleared his throat. "Hattie and I have been together the best part of sixty years." His breathing went shallow, and he rubbed a hand over his heart.

Concerned, Eden gestured him to a mustard-colored vinyl couch and gently eased him down. Surreptitiously, she took his pulse while holding his hand. To her relief, his pulse was strong and steady. "She's going to be all right," she said, praying her words were true. "Would you like some coffee?"

Norman managed a smile. "Please."

"I'll be right back." She walked down a corridor until she found a coffee machine and fed quarters into it. Balancing two foam cups, she rejoined Norman and handed him one.

She took a sip and grimaced. The coffee, as black as sludge and twice as thick, burned its way down her throat.

She made herself take a second sip, then another, knowing she'd need the jolt of caffeine before the night was over.

Norman didn't drink, just wrapped his big hands around the cup. That seemed to settle a little. The tremors smoothed out of his voice. "Thank you."

"Hattie's strong," Eden said, setting her cup aside. "She's not going to let a fall keep her down."

His face brightened. "You're right. Hattie's a trouper. Did I tell you about the time she . . ."

Eden listened to a story she'd heard a dozen times before, but she didn't mind. She held Norman's hand, squeezing it when his voice wavered again, pretending not to notice when his eyes filled with tears.

When the surgeon appeared, they both stood.

She thought of the many times the positions had been reversed, when she had been the doctor delivering news, good and bad. She'd understood, or thought she had, the fear, the hope, of what those waiting for news of a loved one felt. Now she realized she hadn't understood at all.

"Mr. Zwiebel," the doctor said, "I'm Dr. George. I've set your wife's right hip. She's still under sedation right now and probably will stay that way for the next few hours."

Norman's hand tightened around Eden's. "Is she . . . is she going to be all right?"

The doctor gestured toward the couch. "Why don't we sit down?"

Eden slipped an arm around Norman's shoulders and helped him back to the couch. The torn vinyl crackled as they sat. He tried to speak, couldn't, and turned to Eden, his face mirroring all he wanted to say.

"I'm Dr. Hathaway," she said quietly. "I'm also a friend of Norman and Hattie's."

"I'm glad you're here." The doctor shifted his attention back to Norman. "Mr. Zwiebel, your wife is going to be all right." He paused. "Eventually. But she's going to need a lot of care, even when she comes out of the hospital."

"That's no problem," Norman said quickly. "I'll take care of her. Just like she'd do for me."

The doctor and Eden exchanged looks. "She may need more care than you alone can give her," he said gently, and he stood. "Look, we don't need to make any decisions right away. It'll be a while before your wife will be able to leave here. Why don't you go home and get some sleep? You can see her in the morning."

Norman struggled to his feet. "Thank you, Doctor. But I'm not leaving. Hattie might need me. We haven't spent a night apart in sixty years. I don't intend to start now."

The doctor smiled slightly. "I'll arrange for a cot for you in her room." He signaled an aide to have her make the arrangements. "Doctor," he said to Eden, "may I talk with you for a minute?"

Eden patted Norman's shoulder. "I'll be right back."

She walked down the hallway with the doctor until they were out of earshot. "Is Hattie's condition more serious than you said?"

"Mrs. Zwiebel sustained a bad fracture to her hip. I don't need to tell you that at her age and with her bones as brittle as they are, she might never recover completely. Someone needs to prepare her husband for the eventuality that she might never be able to come home. She may spend the rest of her days in a nursing facility."

Tears stung her eyes, but she blinked them away. "I think it'd kill Norman to be separated from Hattie."

"Do they have any other family?"

"They lost their only son a few years ago. But they have friends. Lots of friends."

"They're going to need them." The doctor pushed his slipping glasses higher on his nose and sighed. "I've been doing this for thirty years. It never gets any easier."

"Thank you, Dr. George," she said.

After the doctor left, Eden accompanied Norman to Hattie's room, where she'd just arrived from the recovery area. The slight, pale figure in the bed in no way resembled the active, bright-eyed woman Eden knew, and she hesitated in the doorway.

But not Norman.

He crossed the floor to stand beside his wife's bed. Gently, he lifted her hand and pressed it to his cheek. "It's going to be all right, Hattie," he said, tears streaming down his face. "It's going to be all right." He sat by her bed and held her hand, refusing to rest on the cot the hospital had provided.

Murmured voices, the slap of rubber-soled shoes on linoleum, the beep of countless machines—familiar sounds. Sounds that should be comforting. Ordinarily, they would be, but worry for her friends clutched at Eden's heart.

She stayed with Norman until morning. She nibbled on a candy bar and finished her coffee. It was cold now and bitter enough to shock her taste buds.

After convincing Norman to go home to rest for a few hours, she stayed with Hattie until he returned. Then she went to her own home, exhausted, worried, and hungry. But overriding everything else was the warm feeling that washed over her as she thought of the love she'd witnessed between Norman and Hattie.

They were two pieces of a whole, neither complete without the other. Theirs was a love that had lasted more than half a century and was still going strong. A love to last a lifetime. The kind of love she wanted for herself.

Unbidden, her mind conjured up a picture of Adam holding Teddy Connelly, his strong hands gentle as he cradled the baby boy against him. Impatiently, Eden brushed the image aside. Obviously, she was more tired than she'd thought.

She couldn't help recalling the warmth in Adam's eyes when they rested on her, though. Or the tenderness of his touch when he brushed his thumb along her cheek.

Had she misinterpreted his expression as longing? And completely misunderstood his touch?

At his office, Adam reflected on his evening at Eden's. She intrigued him; she provoked him; she scared him more than a little. Most annoying, she was occupying his thoughts to the exclusion of all else.

He wasn't sure of anything except that he had to see her again. After the way he'd bolted from her house, he wouldn't be surprised if she had no desire to see him again. He didn't blame her; he'd acted like a jerk.

A campaign meeting with Russ failed to hold his interest, and, idly, he doodled Eden's name on a piece of paper.

Russ' eyebrows furrowed in an annoyed scowl. "I don't know where your mind is, Adam, but it's obviously not on strategy."

"What . . . oh . . . sorry." Guiltily, Adam looked up to find Russ tapping his fingers impatiently on the desk. "What were you saying?"

Russ gave a snort. "Now that I have your attention, I was saying that we need to push your image as a man of the people. Your stint on the police force helps, but you need something more. Right now, you've got the upper hand, but you're seen as a little aloof, removed from the average person—your family background and all. People are suspicious of what they see as the rich and privileged."

Adam couldn't help his groan of frustration. His family background, his looks, his friends—everything about him seemed to be grist for the media. Everything except what he believed, what he stood for.

Did anyone care about that? He was beginning to doubt it.

"What do you suggest I do? Disown my parents and pretend I'm not their son? I'm not going to spend my life apologizing for an accident of birth." He heaved his shoulders. "Does anyone know that I worked for everything I have? Does anyone *care*?"

Russ held up a hand. "Don't get on your high horse with me, Adam. I know you never took a cent from your parents."

"Then what's the problem?"

"You need to project yourself as someone the common man can relate to."

"Russ, I appreciate what you're doing for me, but I'm the one running for office. Not my family. Not my background. If that's not good enough for you, for the people I hope to represent, then I won't get elected. It's that simple."

Russ let loose with a low string of curses that Adam didn't

bother to listen to. "All right," Russ said at last. "What about this do-gooder you're seeing? We might be able to use that."

"Eden? She's a friend. That's all." Was that the truth? Did he even want it to be the truth?

"What about her involvement in the feeding-the-hungry issue? That's a hot item. Isn't she one of the group moving to start some kind of community garden? We'll play that up, make it look like you—"

"Leave it. Dr. Hathaway wouldn't take kindly to having our friendship used as a publicity gimmick." Adam let a thread of molten steel run through his voice. "Neither would I."

"Okay, okay." Russ gave in with a resigned sigh. "Would it be all right if I arranged for you to attend a Rotary meeting next week? Maybe give a short speech?"

Adam grinned at the uncharacteristic humility in Russ' voice. "Sure."

"Great." Russ gathered up his papers into a messy pile, stuffed them into his briefcase, and slapped Adam on the back. "We're going to win this thing, buddy. Just wait and see. In the meantime, trust me. I know what I'm doing." He gave Adam one last look. "Wear a suit. Make it blue. Red tie. The Rotarians like their candidates buffed, polished, and patriotic."

Adam walked Russ to the door and then closed it behind the man.

He turned his attention back to his desk. He still had a job to do, one he couldn't neglect in favor of the campaign.

He punched the intercom. "Harriet. Hold my calls for the next two hours."

At four o'clock, Adam looked at the next folder awaiting

his attention. He rotated his shoulders in an effort to relieve the tension that had knotted itself into a ball.

One more brief, he promised himself, and that was it. Earlier he'd buzzed Harriet to ask her to order a Reuben on rye from the local deli. It had been delivered hours ago but sat untouched on his desk. He unwrapped it now and bit off a piece.

Russ should see him now, Adam reflected. Wolfing down a sandwich at his desk should qualify him as one of the working stiffs of the world, but Russ Delroy thought in terms of publicity stunts, gimmicks, and sound bites.

Not for the first time, Adam questioned the wisdom of asking Russ Delroy to be his campaign manager. He was too flashy, too slick, for Adam's taste, but his father had recommended the man. Adam had reluctantly agreed, more to bridge the gap between himself and his father than for anything else.

Adam scowled, recognizing what was really bothering him. His relationship with his father, never good, had improved since Adam had decided to run for city council. His father approved of what he viewed as Adam's foray into the political world. He'd brushed aside Adam's assertion that he was running for the council to give something back to Eagleton and its people.

Already his father was trying to bestow favors on him, favors Adam knew he'd be expected to repay by awarding city contracts to Matthew Forsythe's friends and business associates. He'd known what politics was like when he decided to run for office; he just hadn't expected the pressure to be applied so soon and so close to home.

Adam studied the demographics Russ had laid out. The man knew his stuff. There was no getting around it.

Adam looked at the phone, a guilty twinge tugging at his conscience. He'd promised Eden he'd call, but he hadn't. It wasn't from a lack of desire to see her again. On the contrary, he wanted to see her again. Very much.

He turned his attention back to the file he had been studying. A smile of satisfaction rested briefly on his lips.

He buzzed Harriet's office. "Done."

"Do you want messages?"

He thought about it. The last thing he wanted to do was spend the remainder of the day returning calls. Right now, he needed to work off some of the pent-up energy that resulted from confining himself to a desk all day.

"No. Unless there's something urgent, save 'em for tomorrow."

Letting himself out the back door of his office and into the elevator, he punched the button for the ground floor. Minutes later, he was in the parking garage.

He unlocked his car, turned on the ignition, and eased into the snarl of rush-hour traffic. He knew where he was going.

Chapter Four

"I didn't expect to see you tonight," Eden said.

He followed her inside. He was beginning to read her, hearing what she didn't say as well as what she did. She hadn't expected to see him again at all. After the way he'd left a couple of nights ago, he didn't blame her.

He lifted a shoulder, the shrug an unspoken apology. "I should have called first." He brushed his fingers over her cheek, then let them trail down her arm until they linked with hers.

"I'm glad you came." She gestured toward the couch. "Sit down."

She perched on the arm of a chair and looked at him expectantly.

For the first time, he noticed the shadows beneath her eyes, giving her a bruised look that tugged at his sympathy. He'd come here trying to absolve his guilt and had been oblivious to anyone's distress but his own. "Not sleeping well?"

"I've spent some late nights at the hospital with a friend."

He listened while she sketched in the details of Hattie

and Norman Zwiebel. Her voice was strained, as though it were being pulled from somewhere deep inside her, the huskiness telling him more clearly than words how deeply she cared about the elderly couple.

"Hattie and Norman are so much in love. If something happens to one, it happens to the other."

He saw her throat move as she swallowed her worry. He wanted to touch her, to soothe the tension from her face.

"I don't want to even think what would happen if Hattie has to go to a nursing home. They've been married over sixty years and still act like newlyweds."

"Even after all those years," he murmured. How many marriages lasted five years, much less sixty?

"It's *because* of all those years. Hattie's told me more than once that love grows with the years. She and Norman are proof of it."

Adam knew of too many marriages where the love had stopped growing and had turned into something ugly and painful, but he was warmed by the picture she drew of Norman and Hattie Zwiebel. In his estimation, though, theirs was the exception rather than the rule.

Thoughts of his parents' marriage hardened his face. His mother, with her endless charity and social functions, and his father, one of the power brokers of the city, shared nothing in common but a mutual desire to keep up appearances. Adam had learned a long time ago that he was not a son to either but a pawn to be used against each other.

He didn't share those thoughts with Eden. He didn't want to see the compassion in her eyes if he were to tell her the truth about his so-called privileged childhood.

"You almost make me believe in happily-ever-afters," he murmured, more to himself than her.

"You mean you don't?"

He shook his head. "Too much of a realist. But, listening to you, I'm inclined to revise my views."

"I hope so," she said earnestly. "Believing in the good things in life is important. It's what keeps us going during the bad times."

Listening to her, he was reminded again of how far apart they were. She was full of hope, light, and finding the good wherever she looked; his work had too often forced him to witness the dark side of human nature.

Could two such people have a future together? The question startled him. Since when had he started thinking in those terms? He didn't bother to puzzle over the answers. He knew only that he wanted to spend time with this woman who wove love into everything she touched. Perhaps some of her magic would rub off on him.

Eden was the first woman with whom he'd wanted to open his heart. She touched him in a way he was at a loss to define.

"May I take you to dinner?" he asked.

She shook her head. "I'm sorry," she said, sounding as if she really meant it. "I promised to stop by the hospital and spell Norman for a couple of hours. He needs to go home to pick up a few things for himself and Hattie, but he doesn't want to leave her alone."

"What about the nurses? Won't they be around?"

"It's not the same. Norman won't leave her with only strangers to care for her."

"And you're filling in the gap?"

"I want to. I'd have gone to the hospital even if Norman hadn't asked."

And she would have, he knew. Eden seemed to have an endless supply of energy. And love.

How she managed it, he didn't know.

"I'll drive you."

She smiled. "That's a nice offer, but I don't know how long I'll be."

"County Hospital's in a rough section of town. I don't want you coming out of there late at night." Too late he realized how ridiculous that was. She'd worked at the hospital for years.

She favored him with a gentle smile. "Adam, I'm a big girl. I've been taking care of myself for a long time now."

"Let me take you this time. When you're done, call me, and I'll pick you up."

He didn't realize he was holding his breath until she nodded. He expelled the breath.

"All right," she said at last. "I'd appreciate it."

"What time do you want to leave?"

"Norman asked me to come at around seven. Is that all right?"

Adam nodded, relieved she was letting him do this for her. "I'll run an errand while you get ready."

When he returned to pick her up at a quarter of seven, he motioned to a sack on the seat of the car. "I picked up some dinner for you."

Eden opened it, finding a variety of food from a local fast-food eatery. "It smells wonderful." She unwrapped a burger and bit into it. "And tastes even better."

Adam smiled at her obvious enjoyment of the simple

fare. With any other woman, he'd never have considered buying burgers and fries for dinner, but Eden acted as though he'd taken her to a five-star restaurant.

She offered him a fry, but he refused. "I had a quick bite already."

She popped the fry into her own mouth and sighed with satisfaction.

He frowned, remembering their extravagant lunch of a few days ago. Eden was not without sophistication, but she seemed to appreciate this simple meal far more.

"How did you know this was just what I needed?"

"I'm beginning to know you. I figured you'd be too busy to fix yourself something to eat."

"You figured right." She dug farther into the bag and produced a couple of packets of ketchup. Spreading a napkin over her lap, she squirted them onto the burger. "I love burgers with tons of ketchup."

They arrived at the hospital just as she finished the last of the food. She licked her fingers, charming him with the gesture.

"Mind if I come in?" he asked, pulling the car into a parking space. "I'd like to meet Norman. And Hattie, if she's up to having visitors. You've told me so much about them, I feel as though I know them." He took her napkin from her and dabbed at her lips. "Missed a spot."

She looked pleased at his request. "I'd like that."

County Hospital showed its age. Like a proud old lady who had once stood straight and tall, she was now bent with the years and ravages of time. The once white limestone was grayed, the trim in need of painting, the grounds unkempt.

The hospital received part of its funding from the city, but it obviously wasn't enough, Adam thought, as he followed Eden to the elevators. The vinyl sofa and chairs in the lobby were cracked, the walls dingy, the linoleum yellowed.

Once again, he was reminded of how much needed to be done for the citizens of Eagleton. If he were elected, he'd have his work cut out for him. The city fathers didn't like spending tax payers' money unnecessarily. They didn't like spending money, period.

They found Norman Zwiebel pacing impatiently, his rubber-soled shoes making a shuffling sound up and down the corridor. "Doctor has some kind of specialist in there with her," he said, jerking his thumb toward Hattie's room. "Won't let me in. Me. Her husband." His voice rose in indignation.

Eden slipped an arm around his shoulders, leading him to the waiting room and nudging him down onto the sofa. "They need to examine her."

"I know. But I want to be with her. She's probably scared, asking for me." Norman looked up and saw Adam. "Who's this? Your young man?"

"This is Adam Forsythe," Eden said. "A friend."

Norman studied Adam in an unhurried way before sticking out his hand. "Looks like he might do. Pleased to meet you, son."

Adam shook hands and noticed two things. First, the soft color that smudged Eden's cheeks. Second, Norman's protective attitude toward her.

He wasn't surprised at the feelings Eden engendered in the older man. Adam felt the same way himself. Well, not quite the same way, he silently amended. No way were his feelings fatherly.

"How's your wife doing?" he asked.

Norman slumped, seeming to fold into the sagging depths of the sofa. "All right, I guess. She was groggy this morning from the pain pills they've been giving her."

"That's to be expected," Eden said.

"I know," Norman said. "I'm hoping she'll feel better tonight."

Eden touched his shoulder. "Norman, if you want to go home and get those things now, I'll stay with Hattie until you get back."

"I'd appreciate it," Norman said. "Will your young man be keeping you company?"

"No," Eden said quickly. "He was just dropping me off. He'll be back later to pick me up."

"I'd like to stay," Adam said. "If it's all right." For a moment, wistfulness stole into his eyes.

Eden looked from Adam to Norman and back to Adam again. "If you're sure."

Norman brightened visibly. "It'd do Hattie good to see you two young people together. It'll remind her of the days when we were sparkin'."

"But Adam and I aren't . . . that is, we don't . . . I mean . . ." Eden broke off the jumbled stream of words and sent a warning glance at Adam.

"What do you mean?" Adam asked, mischief lighting his brown eyes with gold.

"We're just friends," Eden said at last, glaring at him.

She watched as Norman and Adam exchanged man-to-man looks that effectively excluded her.

"Well, be that as it may," Norman said, "it'd still do Hattie a world of good to see you two together. She needs something to keep her mind occupied. You know, she's been wanting to see you get hitched for a long time, Doc. Many's a time she's said to me, 'Doc Hathaway needs a man and babes of her own to care for.'"

Eden could feel the blush creep from the base of her neck up her face. She shot a glare at Adam, who was trying to stifle a grin. He wasn't trying very hard, she thought, judging from the way his mouth was twitching.

Her grandma would approve. As always, when Eden thought of her grandma, a smile slipped onto her lips and into her heart.

"You'd better go while you can," she said to Norman. "We'll take care of things here."

Norman thanked them both and headed to the elevators, leaving Adam and Eden alone.

"I want to apologize," she said as she and Adam made themselves comfortable on the couch.

"What for?"

She gave him an exasperated look. "For what Norman said. He's obviously under a lot of strain and was rambling. People tend to do that when they're worried."

"Norman has every cause to be worried, but I don't think he was rambling. I think he showed a lot of insight."

Eden was saved from responding to that by the appearance of the surgeon.

"Dr. Hathaway, it's good to see you again." He looked about. "Did Mr. Zwiebel go home?"

"He wanted to pick up a few things for himself and Hattie. How is she?"

"Much better than I believed possible," the doctor said, scratching his head. "By all rights, she ought to be feeling pretty low, but she's already started to give me a hard time about letting her out of here." He gave an admiring shake of his head. "She's a remarkable woman."

"May we see her?" Eden asked.

"For a little while. She still tires easily, but she could use the company. That woman can talk like no one I've ever met. When she found out I was single, she told me to find a nice young woman and settle down."

Adam and Eden chuckled.

"I'll see you later," the surgeon said, already bent over his clipboard and walking away.

Eden knocked on the door jamb and received an impatient, "Come in."

She opened it and found Hattie propped up in bed. She seemed in good spirits. The lines of time fanning out from her mouth no longer drooped but rose, as her eyebrows did. "You're spoiling me with your visits." She fixed her gaze on Adam. "Who's your friend?"

Eden made the introductions, blushing again at Hattie's open scrutiny of Adam.

"Glad to meet you, Mrs. Zwiebel," Adam said, taking the hand she offered. It was thin, marked with age spots, and surprisingly strong.

"Sit down, sit down," Hattie ordered, trapping his hand in hers. "Make yourselves comfortable, and stay a while. Doc Hathaway, you've been an angel to sit with Norman and me the last few nights, but we don't expect you to babysit us every night."

Eden moved closer. "I like being here, Hattie. You know that."

"I know," the older woman said. "I also know you need to get out with young people more, not spend your evenings cooped up with two old geezers like us."

Before Eden could object, Hattie turned her attention to Adam. She had yet to release his hand. "Tell me about yourself, young man."

Her unabashed welcome warmed him into a smile, but her inquiry had him sending a look of appeal to Eden, which she ignored. She sent him a you're-on-your-own grin.

He retaliated by resting his free hand on her shoulder. He felt her startled awareness, heard her quick intake of breath.

She wasn't indifferent to him. That knowledge bolstered his courage, and he weathered Hattie's frankly curious gaze.

Adam knew he was being vetted to see if he was worthy of Eden's attention. He felt he must be doing all right, for Hattie smiled widely and patted his hand.

He liked that she felt protective toward Eden. Now all he had to do was to convince Hattie—and Eden—that she didn't need protecting. At least not from him.

"I'm thirty-one, of sound mind and body, and have all my own teeth."

Hattie chuckled. "Can you dance?"

"Yes, ma'am. And, meaning no disrespect, if you were up and about, I'd ask you to go dancing with me, husband or not."

"Full of spit and vinegar. Just like Norman was at your age." Hattie winked broadly at Adam. "Still is."

"Adam and I are just getting acquainted," Eden put in. "He's interested in the Grow a Garden, Grow a Child project."

Hattie leveled a disappointed look at Adam. "Well, I can't fault you for giving a hand with a worthy cause, but if that's all you want with our Eden here, then you're not the man I took you for."

"With all due respect, ma'am, I am interested in the project. I want to see it come about almost as much as Eden does. But that's not the only thing I want."

"And what would the other thing be?"

"I want to date the good doctor." He put out his hands in a gesture of appeal. "Care to put in a good word for me?"

Hattie grinned. "I like him," she said to Eden. "Don't let him get away."

Eden noticed Adam's shoulders shaking. He was enjoying this a little too much. "Hattie, I appreciate your interest, but—"

"Shush, girl. I want to hear more about your young man." She gave Adam a keen look. "Haven't I seen your picture somewhere?"

"Adam's running for city council," Eden said. "You've probably seen him on television and in the papers."

Hattie snapped her fingers. "That's it. You planning on doing something for the city or just sitting on your duff like those good-for-nothings we've got in there now? Bunch of pantywaists, if you ask me."

Eden started to protest, when Adam cut in. "I'm planning on doing everything I can to make Eagleton a city to be proud of."

"See that you do. Or you'll answer to me."

"Yes, ma'am," he answered meekly.

Hattie jabbed him in the chest with a bony finger. "There's a hospital potluck on Saturday. Won't be as good as usual because I won't be there to bring my fried chicken. But the rest of the ladies cook passable. I want you to bring the doc. She doesn't get out enough. Not near enough. Do her good to be squired around by a handsome young buck like yourself."

"I'd be happy to oblige, ma'am."

"Just a minute," Eden said. "Don't I get anything to say about this?"

"No," Adam and Hattie said in unison.

Hattie patted Adam's hand. "You're a right 'un, all right. Just like my Norman. He was a pistol in his day. Still is."

Eden started to read Adam the riot act, when she saw Hattie's face. Laughter had replaced the pain and worry in her eyes. For that alone, she could forgive Adam anything.

Well, almost anything, she amended as she watched the way he and Hattie put their heads together, discussing something in low voices. Just what were they cooking up?

Soon Adam and Hattie were trading stories and exaggerations like old friends. Eden had taken a backseat, content to listen and put in an occasional word.

He was actually very sweet. He had no business being sweet, she thought a trifle resentfully. How was she ever going to keep this . . . this *thing* between them in perspective when he continued to do nice things like bringing her dinner and being sweet to Hattie?

Why, oh, why, had she consented to his driving her to the hospital? That had been a mistake of monumental proportions, and then, what had she done to top it off but allow her heart to melt a bit when he flirted gently with Hattie.

Before she could consider the ramifications of what had transpired in the last hour, Norman returned. Immediately he crossed the room to kiss Hattie. "Look at you. You're prettier than you were when I first laid eyes on you at the cotillion at the old courthouse. You wore a pink dress. Had a matching bow in your hair."

Hattie gave a soggy sigh.

Eden felt tears crowd her eyes. Hattie and Norman had that effect on her. She dug in her purse for a tissue and dabbed at her eyes, hoping no one would notice. When she looked up, she found Adam's gaze on her.

"Something in my eye." She was horrified to find that her voice quavered. Why couldn't she control her emotions? It wasn't like her to be so undisciplined, especially in front of someone who was little more than a stranger.

Only Adam didn't feel like a stranger, she thought. He felt like a friend, a friend who could become something more. Much more.

"Something like how Hattie and Norman make you feel," he corrected softly. "Don't be ashamed of your feelings." He touched her cheek, tracing the trail a tear had left. "Or your tears."

"I'm not ashamed," she muttered. "Just embarrassed."

"Not on my account, I hope."

She darted a glance back at Norman and Hattie. They were so wrapped up in each other that they weren't paying any attention to her and Adam.

"Maybe we should go," she whispered.

They made their good-byes with promises to return soon.

"Eden, you bring Adam back with you when you come again, you hear?" Hattie said, the smile on her face as bright as a birthday candle. "He's a corker. And, Adam, come by anytime. You're good for an old woman."

"I'd be happy to visit you, Hattie," he said, stooping to drop a kiss on her forehead. "But I don't see any old women here."

Her laughter followed them out the door.

In the hallway, Eden turned on him. "Why did you encourage Hattie to think we're . . . we're . . ."

"We're what?"

"Seeing each other."

"Aren't we?"

"No. At least, not the way she thinks."

"What way are we seeing each other?" he asked, his somber voice teasing a smile from her.

"The way friends see each other," she said primly.

"Oh. Does that mean you're taking back the invitation to the hospital's potluck dinner?"

"No. Hattie would never forgive me if I told her you didn't come."

"Is that the only reason you want me to come?" he asked, reaching around her to push the elevator button. "Because of Hattie?"

"Yes." The lie tasted sour on her tongue. "No." She took a deep breath.

"Why?"

"For me."

She was scarcely aware when the elevator arrived and he gently pushed her inside.

"Was that so hard?" he asked.

She didn't trust her voice, could barely manage a nod. She needed time to think. His nearness wasn't helping. It wasn't helping at all.

"Then let me make it easier." Emotion darkened his eyes as he lowered his head to kiss her right there in the elevator. Very sweetly. Very softly. Very insistently.

The kiss didn't ask; it demanded. It stole the air from her lungs and turned her knees to mush.

Her vision blurred. Her mind scrambled.

The world had stopped, save for this moment, this man. All she could think of was what he was doing to her. And how he made her feel.

Just a week ago she had thought her life rich and rewarding—she still thought it so—but Adam fit into it with frightening ease. He was turning her feelings inside out.

She gave and, in giving, received. The kiss deepened, filling her with a quiet warmth.

The elevator reached the ground floor. The door opened. And Adam continued to kiss her. When he raised his head, a smattering of applause greeted them.

He lifted his head. "You see? I've got supporters."

"What you've got is a lot of nerve." But the smile she shot him took any sting from the words.

On the drive home, Eden thought about Adam's question.

The kiss didn't make things any easier. If anything, it made them more difficult, and she almost told him not to come to the potluck after all.

But something stopped her.

Something like the way he looked at her . . . as if she were the most beautiful woman in the world. Eden had no illusions about herself. With her reddish hair and blue eyes, she was passable looking. That was all.

Under her porch light, he drew her to him once more, but this time she pulled away from the hands that gently held her. She couldn't chance another kiss. Not when her feelings were in such turmoil. "It's getting late."

"What time is Saturday's potluck?"

"Sixish or so. We're not real punctual about starting on time." She gave an apologetic smile.

"One more question. Just what exactly is a potluck?"

"You've never been to a potluck dinner before?"

He shook his head. "'Fraid not."

"Everybody brings something to share."

"A bottle of wine?"

"The ladies' auxiliary provides the drinks. We're having lemonade." She laughed at his expression. "You don't have to bring anything. I'll bring something for both of us."

She expected him to share her smile, but his expression sobered as he looked at her, and once more he surprised her.

"I'll be bringing the most beautiful woman there."

Tears sprang to her eyes, and she blinked them away. She'd already cried in front of him once tonight; she wasn't about to do it again.

Adam touched his lips to hers, then left.

Only when she heard the engine of his car roar to life did she realize she was still standing on the porch. And she realized there were no shadows looming across her heart tonight.

Chapter Five

By Saturday morning, Eden was congratulating herself on inviting Adam to the hospital potluck. He'd take one look at the hearty but plain fare served up by the ladies' auxiliary and run as fast as he could. She pushed away the stab of disappointment and told herself it was for the best.

Adam was prime rib and Merlot; she was pot roast and fruit punch. Just one of his custom-tailored suits probably cost more than what she'd paid for her first car.

Still, she didn't really pacify herself with the old chestnut that they came from different worlds. Her education and training were impressive, her job a respectable one, if not particularly well-paying. So why was she trying to push Adam away?

Was she still allowing her ex-fiancé to mess with her mind?

She'd met Jeff nearly three years ago. A loan officer at a local bank, he'd literally swept her off her feet. She hadn't been looking where she was going when she ran into him. Strong hands had caught and steadied her. Over coffee, he'd invited her to dinner.

Instant attraction plus the fact that she hadn't had a date in more months than she cared to count had prompted her to accept.

When she began dating him, she knew he didn't understand her commitment to her work. He treated her long hours and dedication with a grudging tolerance that she'd expected would eventually grow into respect. When he asked her to marry him, she believed he'd finally accepted and embraced the whole of her.

She'd worn the engagement ring and started making plans for the future. Only when they discussed where they'd live once they were married did she realize she'd been fooling herself.

"Once we're married," he said, "we'll start saving for a new house, something closer to civilization. I'm not staying in this burb forever. I intend to move up, and I want you with me, babe." He kissed her lightly.

"Jeff, I have a job here."

"Come on, sweetie. You know what I mean. It's great that you want to work for now, but you can't want to do it forever. Doctoring sick kids?" The curl of his lip conveyed his distaste.

Had she only then noticed how weak his chin was, the ingratiating way he smiled when he wanted his own way?

"Why wouldn't I?"

He had tried to talk her out of it. When he saw that she wouldn't budge, he'd sulked like an ill-mannered child. At that moment, she returned his ring.

She shouldn't have been surprised. Jeff had always put things above people. Position above hard work. She'd let his good looks and easy manner blind her to that. She'd shed her tears in private and vowed never to be that vulnerable again.

After two days of moping, she admitted that her pride had taken a bigger beating than her heart. She had not regretted her choice since.

Grandma had never liked Jeff. She hadn't said a word to Eden, but her disapproval was in every line of her face. When Eden had ended her engagement, Grandma had said only, "It's about time you came to your senses."

Gram had retired to Arizona a year ago with plans to learn to ride an all-terrain vehicle. She embraced life, squeezing out every bit of pleasure. It was a lesson Eden was still learning.

Eden spent the morning baking a huge chocolate cake, her and Adam's contribution to the potluck. By afternoon, she was at the hospital, helping set up long folding tables.

"You shouldn't be doing that," Mr. Cheston, who worked as the maintenance man, said. "A tiny thing like you." He lifted one side of the table.

She hefted the other and propped open the legs. "I can handle it if you can."

He grinned. "Guess you can at that."

They worked together setting up a dozen more tables.

"Heard you were seeing a young man," Mr. Cheston said, elaborately casual.

Eden bit back a sigh. News traveled at the speed of light on the hospital grapevine. No doubt it had started with Norman Zwiebel and been embellished along the way. She wouldn't be surprised if the gossip had her married and expecting her first child by now.

"I 'see' lots of people."

He gave her a reproachful look. "No need to get uppity, Doc. You know we're just looking out for you. A woman alone needs someone to look out for her. It don't hurt a man to know a lady's got people who care about her. Keeps him on his toes."

A smile slipped past her annoyance. She couldn't mistake the interest in his eyes for anything but genuine caring and concern. "I know. I'm sorry."

"That's all right. A woman in love is entitled to be a little touchy."

"I'm not—" She stopped at his knowing smile.

When the ladies of the Hospital Auxiliary League arrived to decorate and set the tables with foam plates and plastic utensils, Eden had heard a dozen different versions of how she'd met "her young man," none of which came anywhere close to the truth. Questions ranged from what his intentions were to how soon they could expect a wedding.

Eden managed to hold on to her sense of humor throughout the gentle but thorough inquisition, but she was feeling sorely tried by the time she reached home.

"Adam Forsythe, this is all your fault," she muttered.

She poked a finger at the newspaper that featured a picture of the man on the first page. The paper was a couple of days old, but she'd saved it, telling herself she hadn't had a chance to finish reading it. She conveniently dismissed the fact that she rarely read the paper completely through.

She spent the next half hour showering and washing her hair. When Adam arrived to pick her up a few minutes before six, she was dragging a comb through her still-damp hair.

"Not every woman looks gorgeous with wet hair," he said, twirling an errant curl around his finger.

Her earlier exasperation with him faded at the warmth in his eyes. She couldn't stay angry at this man. Not for long, anyway.

"I hope you're ready for the twenty-first-century version of the Inquisition."

He cocked an eyebrow. "Care to explain that?"

"I'll let you find out for yourself."

"You're a hard woman, Eden Hathaway," he said, helping her with her coat.

"And you're not getting anything more out of me," she said, laughing up at him. She was still chuckling as she retrieved the cake from the counter. "Ready."

The hospital grounds had been transformed for the up-coming holiday season with miniature lights strung from trees and lampposts.

After introducing Adam to a few people, Eden took her cake to the kitchen. When she returned, she found him talking to Mrs. Longstreet.

Eden groaned. Mrs. Longstreet was the biggest gossip in the whole community. She also had a heart to match her mouth, so everyone tended to overlook her gossip.

Still, Eden didn't want the older woman to get her hooks into Adam. She needn't have worried. Adam parried Mrs. Longstreet's questions with practiced ease and actually had the old lady giggling like a schoolgirl.

"How'd you do that?" Eden asked when Mrs. Longstreet took herself off, declaring she had to see an old friend.

"Easy. I just told her she'd make a great TV journalist. It's the truth. She's got a reporter's instincts—goes right for the jugular."

Eden gave a rueful smile. "Don't I know it."

Eden's hair looked gilded under the hospital's fluorescent lights, a gleaming cap of fire. It lit up her face, highlighting the smattering of freckles across her nose and cheeks. Once more Adam thought of the differences between them— sunshine and shadow.

It was pure pleasure just watching her. He longed to kiss each of the golden freckles.

He heard the laughter in her voice and felt a matching rumble in his chest. He leaned over, brushing his lips across her hair.

"I like your perfume."

"It's shampoo."

"On you it smells like Chanel No. 5."

"Maybe you'd better schedule yourself for a checkup, Mr. Forsythe, with a doctor."

"I'm with a doctor," he pointed out.

"I meant an ENT."

"Hey, my nose works great." He gave her a leer. "So do my eyes. And they like what they see."

She swatted his arm. "The *E* stands for *ears,* you idiot."

He contrived to look offended.

She darted a look around at her friends and colleagues, wondering what they were thinking of her and Adam Forsythe together.

"Let's give'em a real show," he whispered, catching her nervous glance. He kissed her on the lips. The kiss, which he'd intended to keep light and easy, lingered, deepening until he forgot about the crowd surrounding them, forgot he was in the hospital cafeteria, forgot everything but the woman in his arms. Most in the hospital crowd were fairly liberal, but Eden didn't think they were liberal enough to accept their children's doctor's being kissed right there in County's cafeteria.

Startled into awareness by a round of applause, Adam looked up, dazed. Kissing Eden had short-circuited his brain.

"I should go help," Eden said breathlessly. "I'm on the serving committee."

"Is there any committee you're not on?"

She started to smile, then realized what his question implied. "Quite a few, actually."

Adam followed her to where a line of people snaked back and forth upon itself.

Eden slipped behind the serving table and fished a ladle from where it had disappeared into the punch bowl. She looked up to find Adam beside her.

"You should get in line," she told him. "I'll probably be here for a while."

"I'm right where I want to be. Just tell me what to do."

"How are you at dishing out chili?" She pointed to a simmering pot.

"I think I can handle it."

She gave him another ladle. "Get ready. We're about to be descended upon."

The people came, eager to share in the bounty of food that spilled across the table but even more eager, Adam realized, to get an eyeful of the man their favorite doctor was dating.

Eden sent Adam a sympathetic glance, wondering if he knew he was about to be put on public display.

He knew, all right. The look he gave her was half-resigned, half-amused.

"Think I'll pass muster?" he whispered.

In his Dockers and a navy knit shirt, he more than passed. He looked terrific.

"You'll do."

He put a hand to his heart. "Be still."

She started ladling out punch, all the while keeping an eye on Adam. She needn't have worried. After a few false starts, he wielded his chili ladle with panache.

She kept waiting for him to look out of place in the humble surroundings of the hospital cafeteria. Out of place with her.

"Where'd you find him?" Mrs. Longstreet asked Eden in her booming voice. "He's a hunk."

Eden glanced at Adam. Had he heard? Mrs. Longstreet was a dear, but she was notoriously hard of hearing. Vanity prevented her from wearing her hearing aids, so she tended to shout all her remarks, assuming that others suffered from the same affliction.

"He's just a friend," Eden whispered back.

"Honey, men who look like that are never just friends." The old lady winked slyly and tapped Eden on the wrist with her fork. "Don't let him get away. You're not getting any younger, you know."

Eden supposed she should be offended, but she had other worries. Had Adam heard? She chanced a look at him. What she saw in his face confirmed her fears.

He grinned. "Don't worry. I'm not going anywhere."

"I'm sorry—"

"Don't be. I'm glad she approves. Maybe she'll put in a good word for me."

They continued serving until they were relieved by an older couple who shooed Adam and Eden away.

"Take your young man and go sit down," the wife told Eden. "I'll fill some plates and bring them to you."

Eden had long since given up explaining that Adam was not her "young man" and smiled gratefully. "Thanks."

She and Adam squeezed chairs in at one of the long tables. The food was plentiful but plain, and she wondered what Adam thought of it.

There was Mrs. Tyler's tuna casserole, Mrs. Longstreet's chicken pot pie, Mrs. Potter's green beans topped with cheese and crackers, Mrs. Johansen's fish and chips, Mrs. Gibson's red velvet cake, Mrs. Lancaster's pecan pie . . . the list went on and on.

Each woman had her own specialty and was eager to show it off. The good-natured rivalry was part and parcel of the potluck. An empty pan at the end of the evening signalled a success, while a nearly full one was cause for sympathetic glances.

"Thanks," Adam said when a plate overflowing with food was placed before him. "It looks great." He turned beseeching eyes toward Eden and whispered, "How am I supposed to eat all this?"

"You can't. Just make sure you try some of everything."

He picked up a drumstick—Mrs. Harvey's fried chicken—bit into it, and sighed in appreciation. "Fabulous."

Eden glanced around, hoping Adam was aware that his reaction was being scrutinized by everyone present. She berated herself for not warning him sooner and only hoped he understood the importance of the next few minutes.

He followed the same procedure with all the foods squeezed onto his plate, sampling each one and then declaring it to be delicious, delectable, delightful . . . until she was sure he'd run out of adjectives.

Finally, he pushed back his plate and made a show of loosening his belt several notches. "I haven't eaten this much good food since . . . I take that back. I've *never* eaten this much good food before. And I've eaten in some of the finest restaurants in the city."

The ladies hovering around him preened like peahens.

When they dispersed, Adam leaned over to Eden. "I was telling the truth. Everything was wonderful. But I may never move again."

She patted his arm. "You made their day. Thank you."

"I'm flattered that my opinion is so important, but what I don't understand is why."

"You're new."

"New?"

Seeing that he didn't understand, she added, "Everyone else here has been coming to these things for years. When I first got here, I had to make sure I didn't take any more of Mrs. Longstreet's chicken pot pie than I did of Mrs. Shaunessey's Mississippi mud pie. Let me tell you, I made a few blunders until I caught on."

"It's a wonder you don't look like Mrs. Gibson now," he said, "if you've been eating like this for years."

Eden squelched a smile. Mrs. Gibson weighed at least two hundred pounds and was proud of every single one.

"After my first couple of times, everyone lost interest because I wasn't new anymore. Understand?"

"I'm beginning to. Once I come to a few more of these things, no one will care what I eat, because I won't be new any longer. Right?"

"Right."

Neither mentioned the assumption that he *would* be coming to more potlucks.

The shuffling of chairs interrupted what Eden was about to say next, and she looked around. "I'm on duty."

"Again?"

"Cleanup duty."

"Don't you ever quit?"

She smiled at him. "Why don't you sit back and relax? I'll take care of this, and then we can go. Or if you want to leave now, I can catch a ride."

"No way. I'm under orders from Hattie. Lead me to it."

She surveyed the tables, each holding piles of used plates, cups, utensils, and crumpled napkins. "You're sure?"

"I'm sure."

"Thanks. It shouldn't be too bad. There're five others on the cleanup committee."

Eden started clearing the tables. By the time she reached the kitchen, only Adam remained.

"Where is everybody?"

"I sent them home. We don't need them."

She sent him a doubtful look. "Have you ever cleared up after a hundred people before?"

He gave her an unrepentantly cheerful grin. "No."

She sighed. "I was afraid of that."

"Do I get an apron?"

Eden watched as Adam donned an old-fashioned bib apron with ruffles. He shouldn't have looked so appealing, so masculine. He should have looked ridiculous.

Instead, he was more handsome than ever, the ruffles enhancing his masculinity rather than detracting from it. The direction of her thoughts disturbed her.

"You were pretty obvious tonight," Adam said.

"Obvious?"

"Wasn't that the idea? To make me realize that you and I come from different places?"

"Yes." The plan had backfired, though. Adam fit in, charming her co-workers, friends . . . and her. "I thought if you saw how different we were, you'd realize—"

"Realize what? That we come from different worlds?" he repeated. "So what?"

"So what?"

"Yeah. So what? My parents made a so-called ideal match. They had everything in common. Same background, same education, same expectations. Same everything. Everything except love."

"We're not talking about marriage."

"No. We're not. So why can't we see each other? As friends?" He didn't wait for her answer. "We have something special between us, something more important than the differences you feel bound to point out. Can't you feel it?"

"Yes, but it's happening too fast. I don't think—"

"Don't think. Just feel."

Once more, Adam kissed her. It was endlessly tender, endlessly fragile. And so very right.

When he raised his head, Eden stared at him with bemused eyes. Her pulse quickened, and a traitorous banner of anticipation fluttered through her. He gave her a long, steady look, then simply rested his brow against hers.

It didn't matter that they were in a dingy hospital basement, surrounded by the detritus from a potluck supper. It didn't matter that Adam wasn't her usual type of date. Nothing mattered but the man at her side.

"You're quite a woman."

"Says quite a man."

He laughed softly, the sound a comfortable rumble. "Sounds like some kind of mutual admiration society."

"Yeah. We'd better quit before we get really sloppy."

At that moment, all that separated them no longer mattered. All that mattered was how his lips felt pressed against her own.

After long moments had passed, she gently freed herself from the sweet warmth of his embrace.

"Wrong time, wrong place," he said, echoing her thoughts.

Her sigh signalled her agreement. She couldn't bring herself to tell him the truth—that she was afraid to go on seeing him because she was afraid of risking her heart.

They finished cleaning up the kitchen, but the easy camaraderie they'd shared earlier was gone.

Adam took her home, as attentive as always, but she sensed he was far removed, in a world of his own. Perhaps he, too, was having second thoughts.

She wasn't supposed to moon over a simple kiss. Wasn't supposed to yearn over it. Most especially she wasn't supposed to ache over it.

Eden had been drawn to Adam from the beginning. Now she was very much afraid that she could all too easily fall in love with him. Given her miserable track record with men, that would be incredibly stupid. Adam wasn't the kind of man a woman could easily forget.

Not since she'd ended her engagement to Jeff had she allowed herself to feel anything for a man. Even now, almost two years later, she could remember the pain. Jeff had wanted her to give up her work once they were married. She'd tried to convince him that being a pediatrician wasn't just a job; it was a calling.

He wanted a wife, a helpmate, a mother for his children, he'd told her. He'd almost convinced her it all made sense until she realized what he really wanted was a hostess for his parties and respectable arm candy while he entertained his business associates. He hadn't wanted a wife; he'd wanted a Barbie doll.

She shoved memories of Jeff from her mind and prepared for bed. Shaken by Adam's kisses and her response to them, she stayed awake far into the night, still trapped in the feelings Adam aroused within her. He was getting too close, making her feel things she'd thought long buried.

Eden knew she suffered from an overactive conscience. "You can't fix everyone," Gram was fond of saying.

While Eden accepted the truth of those words, she couldn't turn her back on the need that surrounded her. Her job at the hospital and, now, her volunteer work filled her days.

If she sometimes yearned for something more, she didn't dwell on it. Not that there was time for that anyway, she thought. A frown blunted her eyebrows into a straight line.

After refusing offers from teaching hospitals, she'd accepted a position at the county hospital, where she believed she could do the most good. She'd expected to work hard and long. What she hadn't expected was to fall in love with County's run-down neighborhood and its proud residents.

Together, they were rebuilding that neighborhood. They were making progress, she thought. Most of the residents were older, retired people who refused to leave their homes despite the decay of their surroundings. But an influx of young families, attracted by the renovation efforts and cheap prices, was injecting new life into the community. She had built a life here, one she was proud of.

Adam Forsythe didn't fit in with any of her plans.

"What are you doing to me?" she whispered.

Only the sigh of the wind outside answered her.

Chapter Six

Shoving a folder to a corner of the desk in his home office, Adam stretched and yawned. He'd put in hours of catch-up work. Now he wanted to relax. At one time, he'd have flipped on the television and found a movie.

But not any longer.

Because of work schedules—his and hers—he hadn't seen Eden since the potluck dinner, but they'd talked on the phone every night. At first they'd simply shared the events of their days. Their conversations had gradually deepened until they were now sharing thoughts and feelings.

What Eden really needed was a chance to let go, let loose, he reflected. She gave so much to others that she had little left for herself. She did it so instinctively that she didn't realize how much it took from her.

He knew she was probably tired after teaching a nutrition class to a group of mothers-to-be, so he didn't intend to keep her on the phone for long. He only wanted to hear her voice.

He smiled, thinking she'd make a fortune if she bottled

it. Its soft tones had a way of cutting through his worries and dissolving them.

He let the phone ring again. And again.

He looked up the hospital's number and asked for Hattie Zwiebel's room.

Hattie brushed away his questions about her health and cut to the matter at hand. "You're looking for Eden, aren't you?"

There was no point in denying it. "Yes."

"She's likely downtown."

"Downtown? Why? It's freezing out." A cold spell, unusual for Eagleton's normally mild climate, had sent the temperature plummeting. What had taken Eden out on such a frigid night?

Hattie clucked. "That's why she's there. She's giving out blankets and coffee to the street people."

Adam curbed what he'd been about to say. She had no business being out on streets where muggings rose in direct proportion to the plummeting temperature.

"Where, exactly, would she be?" he asked, trying to hide his growing worry.

Hattie rattled off the names of several streets where he might find Eden. He forced himself to thank Hattie politely before hanging up the phone and pulling on a jacket.

An hour later, he was still driving up and down streets, looking for Eden's death trap of a car. When he spotted it, he breathed a sigh of relief.

He found her handing out blankets and coffee just as Hattie had predicted. Even from a distance, he noticed how she shivered from cold and fatigue. The wind gathered up her hair in an angry fist, then tossed it back into her face.

Eden was indisputably the strongest woman he'd ever known. And the most compassionate. But what about *her* needs? Who was watching out for her, making sure she didn't push herself too far, too hard? Taking the time to pull her away from all her causes so she could reclaim the woman inside?

He maneuvered through a small crowd of people.

It had been raining on and off all evening. When he reached her, he saw droplets of water sparkling like diamonds in her red-brown lashes. He looped an arm around her shoulders, hugging her to him. He cradled the back of her head in one hand and pressed her face into his chest.

He held her as much for himself as for her.

"Adam." She pulled away enough that she could smile up at him. "What are you doing here?"

"Looking for you. C'mon." He laced his fingers with hers and gave a gentle tug.

"Where?" She didn't budge.

"I'm taking you home."

"I can't go home. Not yet."

Adam bit back the impatient words that threatened to spill over. Even as he spoke, rain seeped down the collar of his jacket. "It's freezing out here. Let me take you home. Get you warmed up."

"I'm not going anywhere until I finish." For the first time, there was a whiff of irritation in her voice. And a thread of steely determination that warned him that he was in for a fight.

He'd just spent an hour looking for her, scared out of his mind of what he might find. He was cold, tired, and out of patience. "You're finished."

She shrugged off his arm. "I appreciate your coming to look for me, but, as you can see, I'm fine." Her voice softened. "Now, if you'll excuse me, I've got work to do."

Foggy plumes of exhaled air framed her face as she spoke, a silent reminder of the frigid temperature that was dropping even as they spoke.

"I thought caring about you gave me some say in your well-being." He fitted a finger beneath her chin so that her gaze met his. "Was I wrong?"

She shook his hand away. "You weren't wrong, but I can't stop what I'm doing. Not even for you."

"Why do you have to be the one handing out food and blankets?" He ran a hand through his hair. "You can't save the world by yourself. Aren't there others who could do this?"

"If I don't do my part, how can I ask others to help?"

"Your business is healing people, not risking your neck to feed them."

She brushed a cold-reddened hand across his jaw. "I can't heal when those people are starving."

"You need a keeper." He regretted the words as soon as they were out of his mouth and started to apologize, when she stopped him.

"It's lucky I'm not asking for your approval." She lifted her chin a notch higher.

"If you think I'm going to let you wander around these streets alone at night, you're even more naive than I thought."

"How're you going to stop me?"

He tried a different tactic. "Why do you have to do this all by yourself?" he asked again, gesturing to the sacks of sandwiches and blankets that surrounded her. "Aren't there other volunteers who can help?"

"Not many people want to hang out in this part of town."

"I don't blame 'em," he muttered.

"Neither do I. But that doesn't change what needs to be done."

"What's so important that you have to be down here in the middle of the night? Let me take you home, and we'll come back first thing in the morning. What difference is a few hours going to make?"

"Look around you, Adam. Take a good, hard look."

Adam let his gaze take in the scene before him. A mixed collection of people huddled against an abandoned warehouse, seeking shelter from the wind. The miserable building provided paltry shelter, its concrete walls blackened with age and soot, pockmarked with graffiti and obscenities.

A small girl huddled close to her mother, with only a blanket shared between them to shield them against the caustic bite of the wind. An old man cupped his hands around a Styrofoam cup of coffee, the steam haloing his uncovered head. Two teenage girls eagerly accepted the sandwiches Eden handed them.

He swallowed hard. She was right. These people needed help *now*. Not when it was daylight, not when it was warmer, not when it was convenient.

But now.

He was shamed by his tunnel vision. Oh, sure, he could make excuses, telling himself he was worried about Eden, but the truth was, never once had he bothered to really look around him.

Once again, he was humbled by her willingness to do what had to be done, despite the risks involved. He looked at Eden again and saw the compassion, the pity, in her eyes. The compassion was for the people so obviously in need, the pity for him. The realization stunned him.

Each would move her, push her to keep trying, to make a difference, for others, for him. It was one of the reasons he loved her, that huge capacity for giving harnessed to a hard streak of practicality.

She had such humanity inside her that he often wondered how she could bear the weight of it. He, who had spent only minutes here, felt burdened by what he was witnessing. How much easier it was to turn away, to chalk up the misery he was seeing to one of the many tragedies in the world, one removed from his own comfortable existence.

He wondered if Eden allowed anyone else to see that she suffered along with those she tried so valiantly to help. If she'd been able to, he had no doubt that she would have hidden it from him as well. Even when it terrified him, he admired her for her compassion. He knew she must face her professional work with the same courageous determination she brought to her volunteer efforts.

Adam was no stranger to the darker side of life, the streets that reeked of hopelessness and despair. Though as a cop he had tried to help, he'd soon recognized that most problems began far earlier than whatever isolated incident prompted people to commit senseless and often stupid crimes. He'd then worked the system from the angle of a prosecutor. Now he was trying again to help from a different angle.

He had blindly assumed he had all the answers, but he

was learning that there were far more questions than answers.

He saw the people's hunger. More, he felt it.

"What can I do to help?" he asked with unaccustomed humility.

Eden gave him a searching look. "Here," she said, and she handed him a Thermos. "Start refilling the cups. It's instant, but at least it's hot."

"Where are you going?"

"I want to see those girls," she said, pointing to the teenagers he'd noticed earlier. "They look like runaways. Maybe I can convince them to go back home . . . before it's too late."

Adam didn't have to ask her what she meant. Eagleton, like every other city, was full of kids who had left their small-town or rural homes, looking for something better in an urban setting throbbing with excitement and drama. Only that something better seldom existed for them.

He watched as Eden approached the two girls, who worked to put on a show of bravado. In reality, they looked scared, ready to bolt at the slightest provocation. He couldn't hear what Eden said to them, but he saw her slip her hand into her pocket and pull out several bills. She pressed them into the hand of one of the girls.

He wasn't surprised at yet more evidence of Eden's soft heart. He already knew that she had more than her share of empathy.

"You gave them money," he said when she rejoined him.

She nodded. "A little. They agreed to go back home. They needed bus fare."

"How do you know they'll use it for that?"

"They gave me their word. That's good enough for me."

Torn between wanting to lecture her on her naivete and kiss her for her generosity, he did neither. He simply drew her into his arms and held on. "You're cold."

She shivered. "A little."

It was only then that he noticed she wasn't even wearing a jacket. "Where's your coat?"

"I don't have one."

"I can see that. What happened to it?"

"Maybe I didn't bring one."

He wasn't buying that. "What did you do with it?"

Her gaze shifted away from his. Gently, he caught her face between his palms, compelling her to look at him.

"What did you do with it?" he repeated gently, though he was pretty sure he knew the answer.

"I gave it to a woman who was coughing so badly, she could barely stand. I wanted to take her to the hospital, but she wouldn't go. So I gave her my coat. I'm not that cold," she said, immediately negating the words by shivering again. "I have other coats," she said when he continued to stare at her. "She needed one. Anyone would have done the same thing."

Not anyone, Adam thought. *Only Eden.* His carefully ordered life had taken a roller-coaster ride ever since he'd met her. She'd given him a taste of a different kind of thinking, of feeling, of being.

He shrugged off his own jacket and settled it over her shoulders. It swallowed her, but it provided some protection from the wind and rain that whipped around them. By now she was trembling so much, she could barely slip her arms into it.

"I can't take your coat," she protested, even as she did so.

"I'll be all right. I've got a sweater on. It's you I'm worried about. What am I going to do with you?" he murmured, rubbing his hands up and down her arms.

"Help me hand out these," she said, gesturing to the rest of the supplies she'd brought.

"You can't be serious. You're so cold now, you can barely move. Let me take you home. I'll come back and finish up."

"I can't leave yet."

"At least wait in the car."

She smiled and shook her head. "With two of us, it'll go faster."

Seeing that he wasn't going to change her mind, Adam helped her distribute the rest of the sandwiches, coffee, and blankets. Though he wanted to speed things up and hustle her home, where she could start to thaw out, she refused to be rushed and had a kind word or an encouraging smile for each of the people who shuffled forward.

Fatigue had settled into the pockets under her eyes, but she didn't betray it by word or gesture. Occasionally she'd turn to him and give him the same smile she bestowed on those who made their home on the street.

By now he was shivering too, but he kept going, all the while his admiration for Eden growing. The lady had guts. More than anyone he'd ever met.

At the same time, there was a delicacy about her that stirred him in ways he hadn't expected. He wondered if she fully understood just how remarkable she was. He wondered what drove her. What caused her to push herself so brutally?

When the last of the supplies had been given away,

Adam wrapped an arm around her waist. "Come on," he said, and he guided her to his car.

"My car—"

"We'll get it tomorrow."

Adam drove quickly, chancing a glance at Eden when he could. "What makes you do it?" he asked.

"The children," she murmured, exhaustion slurring her voice. "I can't bear the thought of children going hungry."

That explained so much, he thought. Her choice of professions. The classes she taught. Her zeal for the community garden.

Her shivering eventually subsided as the heater filled the car's interior with warmth. Her soft, even breathing told him she was asleep.

At her house, he shook her gently. "C'mon, sleepyhead. Time to get out. We're home."

She mumbled something and pushed his hands away.

"Okay. We'll do it your way." He climbed out, rounded the car, and slid an arm beneath her knees and the other around her shoulders. At her door, he paused while he searched her purse for her key. Finding it, he opened the door.

Inside, he carried her to the sofa. After settling her there, he removed his jacket from her, tucked an afghan over her, then headed to the kitchen. In a few minutes, he returned, carrying a steaming cup on a tray. He set the tray on the coffee table and gently shook her awake.

Hair tumbled about her face, her eyes soft and dreamy as she looked up at him. "Adam? Where are we?"

"Home. Drink this," he said, wrapping her hands around the mug of cocoa.

She managed a few sips. "Thanks."

He sat beside her, making sure she finished all of it.

"That tasted wonderful," she said.

"Hot chocolate should never be served without marshmallows, but I couldn't find any." He gave her a long look. "As a matter of fact, I couldn't find much of anything in your cabinets or refrigerator."

She avoided his gaze. "I haven't had time to go to the store."

"You're so busy feeding everyone else, you don't have time to shop for food." He heard the censure in his voice and knew she'd resent it.

He was right.

"I was going to the store tomorrow," she said, a defensive note creeping into her voice.

He set the cup aside and pulled her up. "Come on. It's time for you to go to bed. You're dead on your feet."

"I'm going right now."

"You're sure?"

"I'm sure." As he started to leave, she lifted her hand so that it fit against his cheek.

The palm she laid on his face felt so good, so *right,* that he resisted questioning the gesture, resisted pulling away. He flattened his hand over hers.

"Adam?"

"Yeah?"

"Thanks. For everything."

He brushed his lips against hers. "I'm glad I could help. Get some sleep. And the next time you decide to deliver food in the middle of the night, call me." He tilted her chin up. "Promise?"

"Promise."

"I'll see you tomorrow," he said, and he let himself out.

Alone, Eden reflected on Adam's reaction. He'd been angry, all right. But it had been *for* her, not *at* her. It'd been a long time since anyone had cared what happened to her. Warmed by his concern, she admitted what she'd run from for too long.

Emotional involvement.

Ever since her failed engagement, she'd shied away from any such commitment of her personal emotions. Adam was breaching the wall she'd erected around her heart, chipping away at her defenses with slow but sure strokes.

A tiny smile hovered at her lips. Warm and caring, strong yet gentle, he made her feel cherished. His concern furled around her like tender arms. Her smile dimmed as she realized the implications. She was falling in love with Adam. But was even love enough to bridge the differences between them?

Absently, she stroked his jacket, which he'd tossed on the back of the sofa and then forgotten. The leather was warm and supple beneath her fingers. She lifted it to her face and inhaled deeply.

It bore the scent of the aftershave he favored and another, subtler one. She puzzled over it, until she realized that the jacket smelled of Adam himself. She made a note to return the garment to him.

She was smiling as she got ready for bed. Tomorrow was Saturday. Maybe they could spend the day together. She fell asleep, a tiny smile still on her lips.

Pounding on her door woke Eden. She glanced at the clock: 7:00 A.M. Who would be knocking at this time of morning?

She grabbed her robe and tied it about her waist as she went to open the door.

Adam stood there, his hands full of cartons and containers. "May I come in?"

She stepped back, holding the door open for him. "Sure." Surreptitiously, she smoothed her hair and wondered if her face bore sleep wrinkles.

Adam headed to the kitchen.

"What's all this?" she asked, following him.

"Breakfast." He tugged at one of her curls. "Get dressed in jeans and a sweatshirt. As soon as we eat, we're heading out."

"Where?"

"You'll see."

She went to pull on jeans and a sweatshirt, then dragged a brush through her hair. Adam was pouring orange juice as she walked back into the kitchen.

"Hope you like bear claws," he said, passing a pastry box to her.

"Love 'em. Especially the gooey kind where the frosting gets all over my fingers and I have to lick it off."

He toasted her with a glass of juice. "My kind of woman."

As they ate, Eden studied Adam. Licking icing from his fingers, he didn't look like a serious-minded city council hopeful. He looked happy. He also looked like a man with a secret.

"Where are we going?"

"It's a surprise." The smug grin on his face told her he wasn't saying anything more.

Eden felt a matching grin tickle her lips. She loved surprises.

He helped her rinse the dishes and then held out his hand. "Ready?"

"Ready." She put her hand in his. "I just wish I knew what I was ready *for.*"

"How are you with a paintbrush?"

"Pretty good, I guess. What are we going to be painting?"

"Norman and Hattie's house."

She stared.

"I stopped by County to visit Hattie a couple of nights ago. Norman told me he'd been planning to paint the house before her fall. I thought we'd surprise them."

Fifteen minutes later, they pulled up in front of the Zwiebels' home.

Eden looked at the tiny clapboard house, its once yellow paint chipped and peeling. "If they can't make the house accessible for a wheelchair, they might both have to move to assisted living, which they can't afford."

"We're not going to let that happen." There was nothing idle in Adam's words. It was a promise. A steadfast vow.

"Right?"

"Right." After a minute, she smiled. "You make me believe everything will be all right."

"I know we can't do the whole thing by ourselves. I've got some campaign volunteers coming in to work on it tomorrow. I thought we'd make a start, though."

It was his nature, she reflected, to help an elderly couple he'd just met. To make their house wheelchair-accessible. To turn what could be a chore into fun.

She leaned across the stick shift to kiss him. "You're a nice man."

"Only nice?" He looked affronted. "This is all part of my campaign to convince you that I'm the best thing to come along since sliced bread."

She made a scoffing sound. "A man who brings bear claws at seven in the morning rates way above sliced bread."

"Does that earn me another kiss?"

"I'll let you know when we're done."

Whistling softly, Adam went to haul a ladder from the garage while Eden unloaded supplies from his trunk. "I thought we'd start at the back of the house," he said when he returned to the car.

"Why not the front?"

"We'll get better as we go, and the front will get our best work."

It should have been dull, Eden thought, sanding away layers of ancient paint. But not with Adam. As they prepared to start painting, he swiped his brush down her nose, leaving a yellow stripe. When she tried to wipe it away, he took the rag from her and did it for her. The small gesture warmed her, as did the look in his eyes, a look that promised there'd be more days like this one.

By the end of the morning, they'd completed the back and one side of the house's trim.

"Break time," he called.

She pushed back her hair and gave an exaggerated moan. "Thank heavens. I thought you were going to work us straight through the day."

"Do I look like a slave driver?"

She cocked her head to one side. "I don't know. What does a slave driver look like?"

He pulled his eyebrows together and assumed a fierce expression. "Like this."

She only laughed, causing him to look fiercer than ever.

Adam pulled a cooler out of his trunk and produced cold roast beef sliced paper thin, hard rolls, and spicy mustard. When he discovered he'd forgotten a knife, they used a wooden paint stirrer to spread the mustard.

They took their time eating, enjoying the food and each other.

"We'd better get back to work," Adam said, putting the leftovers back into the cooler. "I've got a strategy meeting with Russ tonight. He thinks we need a media blitz before the election."

"You'll win without that," she said.

"I wish Russ shared your confidence."

She grimaced in distaste. She'd met the man only once, but he'd come across as pushy and full of himself.

"Russ doesn't connect with everyone," Adam said. "But he's an all-right guy. He's worked plenty hard for me."

"Was it for you?"

"What do you mean?"

Eden lifted her shoulders in a small shrug. "He strikes me as someone who's always looking out for number one, always looking for the advantage."

"You're wrong. Russ may be a little overenthusiastic, but he'd never cross the line."

"I hope you're right."

"Russ is a friend of my father's. He wouldn't do anything to hurt me."

By unspoken agreement, they changed the subject.

As Adam had predicted, their work improved as they

went along. Eden was almost sorry when they'd reached the front of the house and were nearly done.

Adam gathered up the brushes and washed them out under the hose while she stood back to admire their efforts.

"I think it looks pretty good," she said.

"It's nice to know I have another profession to fall back on if this city council thing doesn't work out." He checked his watch. "I'd like to take you to dinner, but I've got to get home for a meeting with Russ."

After taking Eden home, Adam thought of their conversation about his campaign manager. Resolutely, he pushed away his own misgivings about Russ Delroy. He felt disloyal even considering the idea of replacing him. But, like a nagging toothache, Eden's words wouldn't go away.

At the strategy meeting, Adam studied the other man.

Russ poked Adam in the arm. "The election's in two weeks. Two weeks to convince the voters that you're the best man for the job."

"I'm not the best man. I'm *a* man," Adam said wearily. He was getting tired of Russ' phony-sounding harping.

"Don't you get it? You're what this city needs. As you always say, you can make a difference. You can do something to help all the people out there who need someone on their side." Russ waved an arm toward the window, encompassing the city beyond.

Some of Adam's annoyance slipped away. "I'd like to think so," he said, thinking of the shelter, the county hospital, Grow a Garden, and all the other things that needed someone to work toward making conditions better. "There's a lot to be done."

"And you're the man who can do it." Russ clapped Adam on the back. "But first we've got to get you elected. The name of the game's exposure." Russ gave Adam a speculative look. "You still seeing the doc?"

"Whether I am or not, it doesn't belong in the campaign."

"Adam, don't you get it? You left yourself open when you decided to run. Anything you do is public property. Seeing a kiddie doc, especially one involved with fighting hunger, is good PR."

"I didn't ask out Eden Hathaway for good PR," Adam said in distaste. "I asked her out because I like her." It was a lot more than liking, but he wasn't about to admit that to Russ Delroy.

"Sure, sure. I know that. But that doesn't mean we can't use it to our advantage." Russ lifted his hands in a what-can-I-do gesture. "I didn't make the rules. I just play by them. And so will you, if you want to get elected and then stay in office."

"No." The word hung in the air.

"But—"

"Eden's a friend. I don't use my friends." Adam picked up the latest voter poll and pretended to study it, hoping Russ would take the hint and let it go.

"Look, Adam, you're a good guy, but you're being incredibly naive if you think you can run for office and not play the game."

"That's the difference between us, Russ. I don't see this as a game."

"No, I don't guess you do," he murmured. He snapped his fingers. "That's it. We'll play up your integrity, your old-fashioned values, and—"

"Russ, I've got an idea."

"Great. What is it?"

"Why don't we let the voters decide for themselves? The people know where I stand on the issues. Let's let them make up their own minds."

"Adam, when are you going to learn?" Russ was shaking his head. "About the doc—"

"Forget it."

"We could use—"

A warning look from Adam had Russ shutting up, his mouth drawing into a thin line.

"Good enough," Russ said two hours later as he and Adam wrapped up the details of a radio announcement.

Adam watched as his campaign manager finally took off.

More and more frequently, Adam was regretting his decision to hire Russ Delroy. Russ was politically savvy, all right, but he seemed to lose all perspective in his desire for a win.

Adam supposed he should be grateful that Russ was so hard-driving, but right now all Adam wanted was for the election to be over. He was tired of the repetitive speeches, the glad-handing, the baby kissing, the everlasting rapid smiling and meaningless chitchat at wastefully expensive parties with the city's movers and shakers.

If only he could talk about all this with Eden. She'd know what to do. But he dared not involve her in any political machinations. No way.

Adam recalled Russ' urgent interest in publicizing his friendship with Eden. But surely his insistence hadn't meant anything. Adam had made it clear how he felt about using Eden or his relationship with her to win votes.

He suddenly realized what he wanted. He wanted more than an evening or two with Eden. Things had a way of tasting better, smelling better, feeling better, when he was with her. For once, he didn't stop to analyze the feeling. He accepted it. He wanted a future with Eden Hathaway.

But by the time he saw the papers the next morning, it was too late.

Chapter Seven

*E*_{*x-cop*} *Adam Forsythe and pediatrician Eden Hath-away* . . . Adam kept reading the news article, his temper heating with every word.

Strictly speaking, the article didn't contain anything that wasn't true. It mentioned his contribution to the Grow a Garden, Grow a Child fund, his presence at the county hospital's potluck dinner, his volunteer efforts with Eden on behalf of the homeless and even the Zwiebels, which Adam had mentioned in passing to Russ to account for his paint-spattered appearance on Saturday night.

But it implied a lot more, making it sound as if Adam had been instrumental in developing the idea of a community garden for Eagleton's poor and was now spearheading the project to completion. It was an insult to all those who had worked so hard to raise funds and interest in the idea.

The whole thing smacked of Russ Delroy's handiwork. Adam's lips tightened as he reread the parts about Eden.

She'd hate this. He didn't find it strange that his first

concern should be for her. His campaign for public office paled in comparison to hurting Eden.

Even as he read, he reached for the phone and punched in her number. With any luck, she hadn't seen the paper yet. Maybe he could warn her before she read the article.

"Eden, it's Adam."

"How good to hear from you. I'm surprised you have time to call, what with all your volunteer work."

He flinched at her sarcasm. He was too late.

"It's not what you think. I swear to you I didn't have anything—"

"I'm sorry." Her voice sounded ragged. No doubt she'd been on the phone answering questions fired at her by over-eager reporters. "I know it wasn't you. I shouldn't have snapped at you like that."

Deep, warm satisfaction spread through him as the sincerity of her words stroked his soul. She believed him. He breathed a sigh of relief.

He couldn't change what had happened, but at least Eden didn't blame him for it. He felt as though a great weight had been lifted from his shoulders, and he allowed himself a grim smile. He'd deal with Russ later.

"I should be the one apologizing," he said.

"For what? It was Russ, wasn't it?"

He didn't answer directly. "It's my campaign. My responsibility."

"You didn't do anything wrong. You couldn't."

Her faith in him warmed him in unexpected ways. "That's just it. I didn't do enough to stop it either. If I had, this wouldn't have happened. I should've listened to you about Russ."

"You believed in your family's friend. That's nothing to apologize for. It's not your fault that he abused your loyalty."

Her voice, soft as a summer rain, washed over him, absolving him of guilt.

"Will this cause problems for you?" he asked.

"I don't think so. I've been on the phone, fielding questions from reporters. The publicity might even help the Grow a Garden fund."

He could hear the smile in her voice now and knew it was for his benefit. Once again he was reminded of her generosity of spirit. She'd been used, their relationship had been used, but she'd managed to turn it into something positive.

"What are you going to do?" Her voice had sobered, forcing his attention back to what needed to be done.

"Get rid of Russ, and get the paper to print a retraction."

"Why?"

"Because he used you, used us."

"I understand that. What I meant was, why have the paper print a retraction?"

He paused, surprised at the question. "I thought that's what you'd want."

"I'm not ashamed of our relationship," she said quietly.

"Neither am I. I just don't want it used as a publicity stunt."

"Neither do I. But it's done now. And the paper can't retract something if it's true, can they?"

"No . . . I guess they can't. But they could correct the impression that I spearheaded the project you've worked so hard on."

"Adam?"

His voice went dry at the sound of his name on her lips. "Yeah?"

"I once told you I wanted you as the spokesperson, the public face, for Grow a Garden, didn't I?" She chuckled wryly. "Well, Russ Delroy just made that happen. So now I should simply thank you."

"For what?"

"For caring how I feel."

"Don't you know how important you are to me?"

"I'm beginning to."

He hung up a few minutes later and read through the story again. He reached for the phone.

"Russ? You're fired."

Without a manager, Adam started handling the campaign, or what was left of it, the way he'd wanted to from the beginning.

He called a local radio station and asked for air time. The night of the broadcast, he phoned Eden, needing to hear her voice before he went on the air.

"You'll be great," she said.

Her quiet faith filled him with confidence. His earlier nervousness vanished as he waited for his introduction.

"Too many of us are expecting volunteers, churches, social programs, *someone else* to take care of our problems." He paused, letting his words sink in. "Well, it's not going to be that easy. *We* have to help—you and me. Our beautiful city has a big stain on it. Here, in the greatest country in the world, people are going hungry. We won't solve this problem by ignoring it or simply throwing a few dollars into a charity tin. There are families, children, who need our help now."

He answered questions and exhorted the citizens of Eagleton to vote their conscience.

At the end of the broadcast, he sat back, weary but pleased.

Eden listened to Adan's broadcast, tears streaming down her face. Adam did care.

So proud she could burst, she drove to the radio station and waited for him outside.

When Adam emerged, he was surrounded by news reporters all shooting questions at him. She edged closer, wanting to hear his answers.

"Mr. Forsythe, can you tell us more about how you plan to help the homeless and working poor of our city?"

"First, by allocating funds for a community garden. Second, by directing funds toward suitable shelters and food pantries, and toward upgrading existing facilities and programs at County Hospital, and by creating more employment opportunities for the less fortunate among us. Third, by making sure that people see that hunger and want among our citizens, our *children,* is *everyone's* problem."

The reporter smirked. "You really think that's going to work? That taxpayers will go for more spending on those things?"

Adam leveled a hard gaze at the cocky, cynical man. "It will work if we all start thinking with our hearts as well as our heads and focus on the big picture, not simply our own apparent self-interest. In the long run, poverty and inner-city hunger affects us all in countless ways."

"So you'll raise taxes?"

"If I'm elected to the city council, I intend to push for a

budget that will help feed and employ Eagleton's needy, starting with funding the community garden so many volunteers have worked so tirelessly for. Of course, money alone isn't the answer. It's going to take *all* of us to make a difference. Someone once told me that it starts with one person, one voice. If elected, I will be that voice in city hall."

Eden's heart swelled with love as she listened to him. He did understand. She waited until the reporters had dispersed and Adam was alone before joining him.

He grabbed her and kissed her.

"You heard the broadcast?" he asked.

She nodded.

"What'd you think?"

"I think you can do anything you set your mind to." She hugged his arm and rested her cheek against it.

Two days later, Eden's words were proved true.

As she tossed a load of laundry into the washer, she heard the radio announcement of the city council election results.

"Forsythe wins by large margin."

She smiled, remembering Adam's last radio interview. He would make a difference in the city—because he cared.

Her smile dimmed as she thought about what his win would mean to their fledgling relationship. Though she was learning that they had more in common than she'd first thought, she wasn't naive enough to believe that all their differences would be wiped away simply because she wished it so. His position on the council might even further emphasize those differences.

She had cause to think about that again when Adam showed up that evening.

He drew her into his arms and kissed her, the quiet conviction behind his kiss more moving than even the gesture itself. When he raised his head, she took a slow breath, trying—and failing—to steady her heartbeat.

"Harry Roberts, one of the council members, is throwing a party to celebrate," he said. "I want you there. With me."

She slipped from his arms. "I . . . don't think I'd really fit in with all those political types."

"You'll fit in beautifully wherever you are," he said loyally. "Besides, you'll be with me. I need you there."

"You do?"

"Absolutely. To keep me from being bored senseless. Harry and Lorraine Roberts throw the dullest parties in town."

"Oh."

"I *want* you with me," he emphasized, sliding the back of one finger across her cheek.

"Yes."

"Yes what?"

"Yes, I'll go."

"You won't be sorry."

Eden prayed he was right.

The night of the party, she'd changed clothes three times before putting on the dress she'd originally planned to wear, a forest green velvet one with long sleeves and a lace collar.

When the doorbell rang, she ran to answer it.

Adam took one look at her and gave a low whistle. "You look fantastic."

"So do you."

In a tux, he was even more arresting than usual. Eden wished it were just the two of them celebrating tonight. She and Adam had had precious little time together, especially during the past few weeks.

When Adam fired Russ Delroy, he'd taken over the campaign manager's duties in addition to keeping up with volumes of his own work as an ADA. She was honest enough to admit she'd missed him while he was so busy, both before and since his election.

Some of what she was feeling must have shown in her face, for he pulled her to him and kissed her lightly. "I know. I'd rather it was just the two of us."

"It's all right."

Adam kissed her again. "We don't have to stay long."

"I don't mind. As long as we're together."

When they were shown into the Roberts' mansion thirty minutes later by a dour-faced butler, she wondered how truthful her words had been.

Laughter spiked the air. The scent of expensive perfumes wafted around her, so cloying and heavy she could scarcely breathe. The clink of crystal and fine china competed with dozens of voices raised to be heard over the live band. The resulting din resembled the chatter of angry magpies.

She smiled wryly at the analogy.

Jewel-toned dresses contrasted with dark tuxes, a paint box of colors and a perfect backdrop for an evening devoted to excess.

They were all there, she thought. The wealthy and influential, the power brokers and those who worked behind the scenes to wield that same power. She put names to faces she'd seen only in the society page of the newspaper.

Adam took her elbow, steering her toward a cluster of people.

"Eden, I'd like you to meet Councilman Roberts and his wife, Lorraine. Harry, Lorraine, Dr. Eden Hathaway."

Eden shook hands, aware of the raised eyebrows and subtle scrutiny directed her way by the councilman and his wife.

"It's nice to meet you," she murmured.

"Dr. Hathaway, how good of you to come," Lorraine Roberts said, barely touching Eden's hand with limp fingers.

"Yes, yes, good of you to come," her husband seconded.

"Doctor, will you forgive me if I steal Adam for a few minutes? I have someone I'd like him to meet." Without waiting for an answer, Lorraine hooked her arm through his.

Adam gave Eden an apologetic look before allowing Lorraine to lead him away.

Eden turned to the councilman. "It's very generous of you to host this party for Adam."

A champagne flute in one hand, Harry Roberts preened a bit. "Told Lorraine to pull out all the stops for tonight's bash. She knows how to throw a party."

Eden let her gaze travel around the room, nodding her agreement. "She must be very organized."

Harry laughed. "She should be. She's got two secretaries who do nothing but arrange things for her."

Not knowing how to respond to that, Eden simply nodded again. "Councilman, I'm glad to have a chance to talk with you."

He smiled at her now, the smooth, urbane smile of a man who knows he can grant—or deny—favors. "Oh? Why is that?"

"It's about finding land for the community garden. Perhaps Adam's mentioned it to you?"

A shadow of annoyance, quickly banked, rippled over his face. "Yes, I believe he did. Sounds like a good thing."

"I'm glad you think so, because we could use your support."

For the first time, his smile faltered. "My support?"

"We hope to have enough money to buy land for the garden soon. If the city council could match what we've raised—"

"Hold on a minute. We're talking about a lot of money here. A whole lot of money."

She needed to tread carefully. "Councilman Roberts, if you could see how many children go hungry, develop diseases from malnutrition, you'd know why the garden and pantry and shelter are so important."

"I've visited the city shelter. It looks very efficient. The director told me they feed over a hundred people a day."

She heard the pride in his voice, the smug tone that told her that numbers, not actual people, would always come first with him.

"I think you're missing the point, Councilman. Those people are at the shelter because they have nowhere else to go. That's why we need—"

"You want even more of taxpayers' hard-earned dollars to go to the shelter?" he asked caustically.

She bit back an impatient sigh. "The shelter alone isn't

the answer. It's a temporary solution to poverty at best. People need ways to help themselves."

Tiny lines of irritation edged his lips. "Everything costs money, Doctor. Honest, hardworking taxpayers' money. We have to take that into consideration. If these people using the shelter had any ambition, wouldn't they be out working, not waiting for a handout?"

Eden tried to keep her words reasonable, her tone even. She wouldn't accomplish anything by giving way to the anger that threatened to spill over at his callousness.

"Handouts are the last thing most people want. They want to work, to feed and take care of their families."

"Then why don't they get jobs?" he snapped.

"Have you ever tried looking for a job, Councilman, when you have children to raise but nowhere to change clothes, to bathe, to brush your teeth?"

"Well, no, but that's not the point."

"It's exactly the point."

"You're being too emotional," he said, the patronizing tone in his voice grating on her nerves. "Natural enough in a woman." He favored her with a condescending smile, the flash of teeth mirroring the hard-edged glint of the champagne flute he held.

"That's right. I am being emotional. But that doesn't mean I'm wrong."

He patted her hand. "You can't change the world overnight."

Her control snapped, and she snatched her hand away. "That's the poorest excuse for doing nothing I've ever heard."

"There are organizations designed to help these people."

"Who exactly are 'these people,' Councilman?" she asked, her voice dangerously quiet.

"People who . . . you know what I mean."

A fierce light glowed in her face, and the heat of it toughened her voice. "No, I'm afraid I don't. Why don't you explain it to me?"

"People who won't get a job," he snapped.

"Have you ever met a homeless person? Talked to one? Found out why he or she is on the streets?"

"Well . . . no. But I don't have to—"

"In other words, you don't have any idea what you're talking about," she interrupted.

"Just a minute, honey—"

"I'm not your 'honey.'" She took a breath, holding on to her control by a thread. "I'm a doctor and a volunteer trying to do something for our community."

"Yes, yes . . . if you'll excuse me, I see someone I must talk to." He turned away, his rotund body bobbing up and down in his haste to put as much distance as possible between them.

She'd bet the good councilman had never known a day of hunger in his life. If she hadn't felt so much like crying, it would have been funny.

It seemed the Robertses weren't finished with her. Lorraine drew Eden into a one-sided conversation, designed, she supposed, to make Eden feel even more inept.

"Now that Adam is a city councilman, you'll probably want to upgrade your image, dear," Lorraine said. "I'll set you up with my hairdresser. I can even take you shopping if you'd like." She gave Eden's dress a disparaging glance.

"Not that what you have on isn't perfectly lovely, but you'll want to find a good designer."

"Thank you for your offer," Eden said in a carefully polite tone. "I'll call you."

"Do." With an airy gesture, Lorraine flitted to a group of couture-dressed women.

Eden stared after her, convinced she'd been examined and found badly wanting.

Adam frowned, searching for Eden in the crowd. She'd been talking to Harry and then disappeared.

He'd sensed her discomfort the minute they walked into the lavishly appointed house filled with politicians, but he'd chalked it up to nerves. Now he suspected that it wasn't so simple. If she was putting up some kind of barrier to protect herself, he was determined to bring it down. She had him to defend her now.

Then he spotted her. Standing slightly apart from the rest, she appeared to be observing the proceedings from a distance. He spent a few minutes just watching her. In her simple dress, with her hair pulled back at the neck and fastened with a silver clip, she stood out from the crowd, reminding him of the first time he'd seen her.

It wasn't just her unaffected beauty, it was something more basic. It was the way she looked at life. Unlike everyone else here, she was happy to get her hands dirty in the service of a cause, and she was not out to impress anyone.

He threaded his way through clusters of people, smiling but shaking his head at those who wanted to detain him. He'd spent the last half hour listening to people who wanted to impress him; now he was doing what he wanted to do.

When he drew closer to Eden, he could see that something was troubling her. Her smile was a little too wide, her eyes a little too bright, as she looked up at him.

He touched her elbow. "What's wrong?"

"Nothing."

"The truth. You're not having a good time." He ran a hand over her hair, as much to comfort himself as to soothe her.

"Who wouldn't have a good time at a party like this? The food's wonderful, the music great, the—" She stopped. "I'm sorry, Adam. I haven't had a heck of a lot of experience with this kind of thing, and I don't really know anyone here."

He didn't intend to let her off the hook. "I thought the Hippocratic Oath meant that doctors have to tell the truth."

She laughed at the obvious inaccuracy but seemed to relent. "All right. But, remember, you asked."

He grinned. "I'll remember."

"After she'd finished with you, Lorraine cornered me. All she talked about was shopping and hairdressers."

"But that's not really what's bothering you."

"No," she said. "It's not."

"Tell me."

"I tried to talk to Harry about the community garden and pantry and all. After patting my hand, he couldn't get away fast enough."

"Sweetheart, not everyone has your social conscience. That doesn't make them bad people. So you don't like Lorraine and Harry, but the rest aren't so bad."

"If you don't mind listening to them take potshots behind each other's backs."

"You're being a little rough on them, aren't you?"

"If you'd take a good look, you'd see it for yourself."

He recognized the truth in her charge. At the same time, he wanted to reconcile two very important parts of his life. He was beginning to wonder if he could.

"Why did you bring me here?" Eden asked quietly.

"I wanted you to meet these people, see what they're like, start to feel comfortable—"

"You wanted me to fit in with them, to become one of them, didn't you? I'm sorry. I can't."

"You're twisting my words."

"Take a look around. I don't fit in here. I almost wish I did, because I know it's important to you. But I tried doing just that for another man. And I promised myself then that I'd never again try to be something I'm not."

"I'm not asking you to be something you're not."

"Aren't you?"

He thought about it. Was he? "*You're* important to me."

"And you're important to me. You once told me I was putting up barriers because of the differences between us."

He nodded slowly. "I remember."

"My not fitting in here represents all those differences. It's up to you whether or not that's a barrier."

Of course he wanted her to fit in with his colleagues, be a part of the social circle in which he moved. "I'm sorry if—"

"Don't be. I'm glad you brought me. We've both learned something tonight. But . . . Adam, what happens to all the leftover food?"

"Leftover food?" He tried—and failed—to make sense of the segue.

"You know, the food that doesn't get eaten. There must be tons at a party like this." She grabbed his hand. "C'mon."

"Where're we going?"

"The kitchen."

Following one of the white-coated servers into the enormous kitchen, she gasped. Dozens of finger sandwiches, hor d'oeuvres, and tarts were piled high on the counters.

"What happens to the leftovers?" Eden asked the man who appeared to be in charge.

The harried-looking fellow whirled on her. "What's the matter? Didn't you get enough?"

"I had plenty. Everything was delicious," she added.

Adam watched as the man relaxed and swiped at his forehead with the back of one hand.

"I'm sorry, ma'am. I shouldn't have snapped at you. You won't tell the missus, will you?"

"Of course not. This must be a very long night for you."

"You can say that again. That is . . . I mean . . ."

"It's all right. I understand." She smiled, a sunbeam of light even though the hour was late.

Adam felt the power of that smile. So did the caterer, he thought, the man looking considerably friendlier now.

"Now, what were you asking about the leftovers?" the white-coated man asked.

"I wondered what happened to them."

"We pitch 'em."

"You throw them out?"

"That's right."

"May I have them?"

"Pardon me, ma'am, but what would you want with a hundred or so leftover berry tarts and toast points with caviar?"

"I know some people who need them. Hungry people."

His face relaxed into a smile. "You can have all you

want. I'll even help you pack 'em up. You some kind of so-cial worker or something?"

"I'm a doctor."

"No kidding? Hey, that's cool."

"This won't get you into trouble, will it?" she asked as they stacked food into fancy pink boxes bearing the caterer's logo.

"Can't think why. I'm glad to see the food go to folks who need it. I never do feel right about tossing out good food. Not when there're folks out there who're hungry."

Eden stuck out her hand. "Eden Hathaway. And you're . . . ?"

"Ernie Silvers. The missus here, she calls me Ernest. But it's just plain Ernie."

"I'm pleased to meet you, Ernie."

"Same here, ma'am."

Adam had kept silent up until then, content to watch Eden work her magic. Now he introduced himself. "Adam Forsythe."

Ernie gave him a long look. "Say, aren't you the guy who just got himself elected to the city council?"

"Guilty as charged."

"You helping the lady here?"

"I guess I am."

Ernie grinned. "I voted for you. The wife liked the look of you. Maybe you're going to work out all right." Despite his smile, his tone made it clear he was still withholding judgment.

They worked quickly, filling a dozen or so boxes. When they'd finished, Eden pressed a quick kiss to Ernie's cheek. "I can't thank you enough. You're an angel."

Color crept up his neck into his face. "Don't thank me, ma'am. I'm just glad to see the food going somewhere it's needed."

"It will," she assured him. She turned to Adam. "You don't have to leave. I'll call a cab and—"

"I'm going with you. You plan on taking this down to the shelter tonight, right?"

"They could use it. Each night, more and more people show up hungry. There's never enough food to go around."

Her heart was always open, he reflected. To her friends. To him. To anyone who needed her. And that open heart lifted him beyond anything he'd ever expected, ever hoped, to become.

"You never stop, do you?"

"I can't help what I am, Adam."

"I wasn't complaining. I was admiring you," Adam admitted.

A month ago, he'd never have entertained the idea of taking party leftovers to a shelter and would have laughed if anyone had suggested it. But, then, a month ago, he hadn't known Eden. A smile traced his lips as he realized how he'd divided his life into two parts—before Eden and now.

He lowered his forehead to hers.

She was unraveling the threads of his life in ways he didn't understand, but he didn't mind at all. "No. I don't guess you can help being who you are. That's why I love you."

Chapter Eight

Eden gaped at Adam. Instant and total shock ran over her face. "You what?"

"I love you." He grabbed her hand. "C'mon. We've got a delivery to make."

"You can't say something like that and then just leave it." *I love you.* The words grabbed hold of her heart and wouldn't let go.

"Something like what?"

"Something like 'I love you.' " Just repeating his words caused her heart to do a long, slow roll.

"Why not? It's the truth." He brushed his lips over hers.

"Adam—"

"I know. This isn't the right place. Or the right time. The story of our relationship." He began carrying boxes of food out the kitchen door.

After they'd filled his car with tarts, finger sandwiches, and hor d'oeuvres, Adam made his apologies to his hosts.

He didn't regret leaving the party early. He'd felt stifled

there, surrounded by people who talked too much and listened too little.

"You can let me out here," Eden said when he pulled up in front of the shelter.

From Eden, he'd learned that the shelter shared space with a community food pantry that also desperately needed funds.

"Uh-uh. I'm staying."

Together, they unloaded the food and carried it inside. The coordinator, who directed both the shelter and pantry, greeted them.

"Is that what I think it is?" he asked.

Eden nodded. "I thought it might come in handy."

"Will it ever. Twenty more people arrived tonight. We ran out of food hours ago. I was just about to go out and see what I could scrounge." He kissed Eden's cheek. "You're a lifesaver. You and your friend here."

Adam stuck out his hand. "Adam Forsythe. Glad we could help."

"Richard Nolan."

Adam started to unbutton his coat, but Richard stopped him.

"You'll probably want to keep that on."

For the first time, Adam noticed the cold. "Can't you turn up the heat?"

Richard and Eden exchanged looks.

"New at this, aren't you?" Richard asked. There was no reproach in his voice, only curiosity. And compassion.

"You could say that," Adam agreed, a chill roughening his skin. "But that doesn't answer my question."

"There's not enough money to heat the building all

night," Adam said. "We turn off the heat after ten and turn it on again in the morning."

"That's crazy. It's seventeen degrees out. And getting colder."

Richard sighed. "Yeah. But who said we lived in a sane world?" He began opening up the boxes of food and gave a low whistle. "What did you two do? Crash a society party and make off with all the food?"

Adam grinned. "Something like that."

For the first time, Richard seemed to notice their clothes. "You weren't kidding, were you? What kind of shindig were you at?"

"We were at a party celebrating Adam's election to the city council," Eden said.

Richard looked at Adam with new interest. "I hope you plan to do something about this." He waved his hands to include the entire shelter.

Adam gave the other man a level look. "I intend to."

The coordinator turned his attention back to the boxes of food. "Our people are in for a treat tonight. I only wish you had some coffee or soup. It'd help take the chill out."

Adam looked at the array of tiny sandwiches, tarts, and hors' d'oeuvres. Fluff. These people needed real food. It was too late to do anything about it now, but that was going to change.

Richard said a few words, and the shelter's residents roused themselves and gathered around him. "Eden, would you lead us in prayer?"

A hush fell over the room, the silence broken only by the whimper of a baby as Eden offered a blessing upon the food.

Adam found himself listening to the words, impressed by their simplicity, their fervency. Murmured "Amens" followed the prayer.

The people began to form a line. Adam marveled at the quiet taking of places. There was no pushing or grabbing for advantage, as he'd experienced at many society events he'd attended. Instead, children and elderly people were encouraged to go first.

"Adam, can you hand out the sandwiches?" Richard asked. "Molly here will help you." He pointed to a teenage girl, who smiled shyly.

To his chagrin, Adam felt a bit uneasy and out of place.

Molly gave him a reassuring glance. Apparently she sensed his awkwardness. "Don't worry. It's not hard."

"Sure. Okay." Adam felt foolish placing the tiny sandwiches on plates, but he and Molly soon developed a rhythm.

"Do your parents often let you volunteer here so late at night?" he asked.

She gave him an odd look. "I *live* here."

He felt as if he'd been kicked in the gut. He stole another look at the girl. She was pretty, with her light brown hair, turned-up nose, and bottle green eyes. Her clothes were worn but clean. She looked like any other teenager. She *was* any other teenager. Except that she lived in a shelter.

"How long?"

"A couple of weeks. I was living on the street until she"—Molly pointed to Eden—"gave me a card with this address."

"Do you like it here?" he asked, and then silently kicked himself. If he'd ever asked a more stupid question in his life, he wasn't aware of it. But he wanted to know. He needed to know.

She shrugged. "It's not bad. Better than the streets. Better than home."

It was the last that made him wince.

"How did you—"

"Enough with the questions, okay?"

"Sure. Sorry."

"Yeah, well, so am I. So are a lot of people. But it doesn't change anything."

No. It didn't change a thing. His sympathy was as useless as the empty words mouthed by politicians who were more interested in vote-getting than in helping.

Unerringly, his gaze strayed toward Eden. She didn't shake her head over a problem, then walk away and conveniently forget it. She threw herself into the middle of it and worked for a solution. Just as she was now.

"Heads up," Molly said. "We need more sandwiches."

Adam speeded up his pace.

His years on the police force had inured him to tragedy. Or so he'd thought. He'd seen the gamut of miseries, what one person was capable of doing to another. But this aching need in a land of plenty was harrowing and heartbreaking.

"Thanks, mister," a small girl said as Adam handed her a plate.

He hunkered down to her level. "You're welcome. What's your name?"

"Jenny. What's yours?"

"I'm Adam." He reached out to smooth back a wisp of hair that had escaped her ponytail.

"I'm glad you and the pretty lady came. Is she your wife?"

Adam looked over to where Eden was holding a baby so that a woman—probably the child's mother—could stand in line. "No," he said softly. "She's not my wife."

"She's nice," Jenny said. "She gave me this." Jenny opened her hand to reveal a gleaming quarter. "Isn't it pretty?"

"Very pretty," he agreed, his gaze still on Eden. He watched as she nuzzled the baby. For a moment, he allowed himself to imagine Eden holding *their* baby. She'd make a great mother.

Something warm, something that felt a lot like love mixed with a large dose of pride, flowed through him.

"I'd better go now," Jenny said, drawing his attention back to her. "Or my mommy will get worried."

"Where is your mother?"

"Over there." Jenny pointed to a thin woman standing back from the people waiting in line for food.

"Doesn't she want to get something to eat?"

Jenny shook her head. "She said she wasn't hungry. But I think she is." Jenny lowered her voice. "She hasn't had anything to eat since yesterday morning."

"Excuse me," Adam whispered to Jenny. He picked up a plate of food, wishing he had something more substantial to offer than fancy finger sandwiches and tiny desserts. He made his way through the crowd to the pale woman Jenny had identified as her mother.

She might have been pretty once, was his first thought as he took a closer look at the woman. Dull and listless, her hair was scraped back, leaving her narrow face defenseless. She might be pretty again, given decent food, enough sleep, and a break from worry.

Too thin, as though the flesh under her skin had been

gnawed away, she appeared ready to drop, but she held herself with quiet dignity, her arms folded across her chest, her head high. The thin sweater she wore was scant protection against the cold, and Adam wondered if she'd accept his coat if he offered it.

Somehow, he doubted it.

"I thought you might like this," he said, offering her the plate instead.

She gave him a tired smile, then shoved at her hair as though to make sure it stayed in place. "Thank you. But I'm not really hungry."

"There's plenty," he said gently.

"The children." She gestured around her. "They need it more. I'll wait."

"You need to keep up your strength if you're going to take care of Jenny." At her astonished look, he smiled. "I met Jenny. You have a beautiful daughter. You must be very proud of her."

The woman's eyes, eyes that looked too old for her slight body and ponytail, brightened for a moment. "I am. She's the one good thing in my life."

"Then you have to take care of yourself. For her." Again, he extended the plate of food.

He must have touched a chord, for she nodded and accepted it. "Thank you. You're very kind."

"No, but I know someone who is." His gaze drifted to Eden, who was still rocking the baby.

"She's lovely."

"Yes," he said quietly. "She is."

Balancing her plate carefully, Jenny joined her mother. "Thank you, mister. My mommy was awful hungry."

Adam watched as mother and daughter found places to sit. No one complained at making room for two more at the already crowded table. There was an acceptance of others here that Adam envied. It all seemed so simple.

There were no divisions by class or race, occupation or education. These people, all of whom had suffered some kind of loss, had bonded together, offering one another the dignity and respect denied them on the outside.

He retraced his steps and once more took his place beside Molly. As he handed out food, he had to pause several times to brush tears from his eyes.

For the first time, he realized how this last lavish celebration party must have seemed to Eden. Trivial. Excessive. And most of all, wasteful. His associates, the ones he'd defended, suddenly appeared as plastic as their smiles, with their petty concerns, jealousies, and vanities.

He had a lot to learn. He watched as Eden now comforted a small boy who had tripped and dropped his plate. At least Adam had a good teacher. A very good teacher.

The director of the shelter swiped a hand across his brow. "That's the last of it."

Adam looked at the empty boxes and said a silent prayer of gratitude that there'd been enough food to go around. This time. What about tomorrow night and the night after that?

"You were pretty good," Richard Nolan said to him, and he smiled. "For a first-timer."

No words of praise had ever meant more. "Thanks." He asked Richard the questions on his mind. "What about tomorrow? Will there be food?"

Richard gave Adam a long look. What Adam saw in the

coordinator's eyes startled him. Pity. Not for the people who came looking for a meal, but for him.

"There'll be some. Trucks from area food banks drop off canned goods twice a week."

"What about bread, eggs, milk?"

"We have volunteers who pick up day-old items from the bakeries, restaurants, and stores."

"Will there be enough?"

"There's never enough. But we make do." Richard smiled grimly. "We don't have a choice."

Once again, Adam was reminded of how little he knew and how much he had to learn. "What will it take to change things here?"

"That depends."

"On what?"

"On you. Me. Eden. And the rest of the people out there."

"One person . . . one voice," Adam murmured. "Maybe it really does start there."

Richard looked at him with approval.

"I guess the trick is convincing more and more people to care," Adam said, thinking aloud.

"You got it." Richard slapped him on the back. "Now comes the fun part."

Adam turned an inquiring look to Eden, who had just joined them.

"Cleanup."

He barely stifled a groan. He was exhausted. It seemed as if they'd been serving food for hours without a break.

"If you'd rather go home, I can always catch a ride later," she said.

Adam looked at the lines of exhaustion etched into Eden's

face. She had to be at least as tired as he was. "No way. I'm staying."

Eden squeezed his arm and gave him a look of such warmth that he wanted to squirm, knowing he didn't deserve it. "My hero."

"Don't."

"Don't what?"

"Don't make me out to be something I'm not. I'm more like Harry Roberts than I realized. I'm selfish, shortsighted, and—"

She put a finger to his lips. "You're nothing like him. You care about people. I saw you with little Jenny and her mother. I *also* saw you slip some money into her pocket."

At one time he would have been embarrassed at having someone witness such an act, but not with Eden. They'd come too far. "She needs it."

"I know." Eden brushed his cheek with her hand. "I'm sorry I took you from your party, but I'm glad you came."

"So am I."

While he did mop-up duty, Adam wondered what would happen the next time a cold spell hit the city, flooding the shelter with more people than it was equipped to handle. What would happen if the food ran out? Would Jenny and her mother have anything to eat at all?

After they had finished, he hustled Eden from the building, ashamed of the relief he felt upon walking outside. He inhaled deeply. Even the frigid night air was preferable to the atmosphere of quiet despair he'd felt inside the shelter.

It was the wee hours of the morning when he took her home. Though they were both exhausted, he was reluctant to end the night. She invited him in for a cup of tea, and he accepted.

While she brewed the tea, he settled himself in the kitchen. Eden was a born nurturer and homemaker. It suddenly surprised him that she wasn't already married and raising her own family.

"Wasn't there ever someone special enough in your life for you to marry?" he asked.

She set out steaming cups of tea, along with a plate of cookies. "There was."

"What happened?"

She didn't answer for a long time. He had just about decided she was going to ignore the question, when she said, "We had gotten to the picking-out-our-china stage when I realized I'd made a mistake. I didn't love him enough. Turns out he didn't love me enough either." She paused.

"He didn't really get me—not the whole of me. He figured that once he put a ring on my finger, he could begin to give me orders on my wardrobe, habits, friends, and career. There were a lot of little things, none of them really important. The fact was, we weren't going to make it work. I gave him his ring back."

Adam wondered at the man who had failed to see how special Eden truly was.

"He was more irritated than brokenhearted, which told me I'd done the right thing." She gave a half laugh. "The truth is, it stung to know I'd done the right thing, because that meant I'd done the wrong thing in the first place. When I told him it was okay for him to tell his friends and colleagues that he'd been the one to break the engagement, he felt much better."

What a jerk, was all Adam could think.

"Last I heard, he married someone whose fondest dream was to be a Stepford Wife."

A laugh escaped before he could push it back, but Eden didn't smile. He sobered, then reached across the table to take her hand. "I'd never do that to you."

Her silence was eloquent, and he knew she was remembering tonight's party.

"I care about you, Adam. More than I thought possible. But I don't know if we're going in the same direction."

"Stop that," he chided her as he helped her wash the teacups. He brushed a tender kiss across her forehead. "It's late. Get some sleep. We'll talk about it another time."

At home, Adam replayed Eden's comment in his mind. Were he and Eden heading in the same direction? The question badgered him through the night, because he had no answer.

Eden shifted the bouquet of gold and purple mums to her other arm and pressed the doorbell.

The whine of a small motor drowned out the sound, and she tried again. Finally, she pushed on the door, finding it open. She sighed as she walked inside. How many times had she told Hattie and Norman that they needed to keep their doors locked?

A smile worked its way past her exasperation as she remembered Hattie's retort: "Friends know they're welcome. If it's not a friend, then we'd better make one of him."

"Hattie? Norman? It's Eden."

There was still no answer.

She was able to identify the noise now—a power saw

ripping into wood. She followed the sound into the kitchen, where she found Hattie, Norman, and . . . Adam. What was he doing here?

"Goodness, Eden, we didn't hear you above all this racket," Hattie said. She tapped Adam on the arm.

He switched off the saw, raised his protective goggles, and grinned at Eden.

"Sit, sit," Hattie ordered, backing up her wheelchair to make room for Eden at the table. "Norman, clear off that chair for the doc."

"That's all right," Eden said. "I just wanted to drop these by and say welcome home, but I can see you're busy."

Norman slapped Adam on the back. "Adam here volunteered to widen the doorways and put in ramps so Hattie can get around."

Eden looked at Adam, uncaring that the love she felt showed plainly in her face. "That's good of you."

He shrugged, clearly uncomfortable with being the center of attention. "It needed to be done. Besides, I think I got a pretty good deal. Hattie's invited me to the next Sunday dinner she cooks."

"That's right," Hattie said proudly. "I may be in this thing for a while, but I can still take care of my menfolk." She wheeled over to pat Adam's hand. "Adam's one of the family now." She looked at the flowers in Eden's hands. "You remembered that I love mums! Norman, get a vase for these."

As Norman awkwardly stuffed the flowers into a mason jar, Eden thought of Hattie's choice of words. *Family.* These days, since her own parents had died tragically young in a car crash and her grandmother had moved to Arizona, she thought of *family* as a collection of people who knew the pleasure of being together and caring for one another for no other reason than that. It took a meshing, an acceptance of one individual by another, differences and all. It took the kind of love and support that didn't demand but simply was.

Eden regarded Norman and Hattie as family in that way. But Adam? Did she feel the same way about him?

Hattie rolled her eyes. "Trust a man to stuff flowers into a canning jar when there's a perfectly good vase in the cupboard."

"I like canning jars," Norman said. "They remind me of your homemade jam."

During the exchange, Adam had walked to stand behind Eden and rested his hands on her shoulders. Now he dipped his head, his breath fanning her cheek.

Eden felt her heart stumble at the love and joy in the older couple's eyes, and she twisted in her chair to look at Adam. She saw the same response mirrored in his eyes.

She held out her hand. When he squeezed it, her heart swelled, and she answered her own question. *Oh, yes.* She definitely felt that Adam was family.

"Can you stay for a while?" Norman asked Eden. "We're going to have lunch in a few minutes. I'm cooking. My five-alarm chili."

"Not today," she said regretfully. "I've got a class to teach. Maybe another time."

"I'll see you to the door," Adam said, still holding her hand.

Eden looked up in time to see the smiles Norman and Hattie exchanged.

"You're a nice man, Adam Forsythe," she said as they walked to the front door.

"It's not a big deal. The Zwiebels needed help making the house wheelchair-accessible so Hattie could come home. Anyone would have done the same thing."

"Not anyone. Only someone who cared. Only someone like you." She sensed his discomfort at her praise and changed the subject. "I didn't know you knew your way around power tools."

"I put myself through school working at construction sites in the summers."

"But your parents—"

"Are my parents. Not my meal ticket."

"I'm sorry."

"It's all right. A lot of people make the same mistake. I may have been born with a silver spoon in my mouth, but that doesn't mean it stayed there."

"No. It doesn't. You never talk about your parents."

He lifted a shoulder. "There's not much to say. We . . . aren't close."

She heard the careful indifference in his voice, an indifference, she suspected, that masked pain. She noticed her hands start to tremble, whether needing to give comfort or to receive it, she wasn't sure.

"I'd like to meet them someday."

"Maybe." Shadows appeared in his eyes, hinting of pain and loneliness.

She wanted to touch him, to comfort him, but she knew better than to offer anything that smacked of sympathy. She turned away, knowing he wouldn't appreciate the tears she felt prick her eyes.

Adam's arms came around her, pulling her against him. She let her head drop into the hollow of his shoulder.

They stayed that way until she turned in his arms, slipping her hands behind his neck. He reached out to feather his fingers through her hair, sending warm, tingling feelings through her. She lifted her gaze to meet his calm, steady eyes and was amazed once again at the strength she read there.

"You're a special kind of man." She dragged her palm down his cheek. It was rough with stubble, creating a pleasant friction against her hand. "Thank you."

"For what?"

"For being who you are. What you are."

"What am I?"

The man I love. But she didn't say the words aloud. She needed more privacy for that. Right now, she wanted to hug the words to herself, savor them. She touched her lips to his.

"Thanks again for what you're doing for Hattie and Norman."

Adam watched as she walked down the path to her car. He put a finger to his lips, still warm from her kiss.

"No," he said softly. "Thank you. For teaching me *how* to care."

He spent the rest of the day installing ramps and handrails for Hattie. The house was small, cramped, and crowded with pictures and memories, a world apart from the white-columned mansion where he'd grown up.

But it was more of a home than the mansion would ever be. It had probably never seen a professional decorator. Hattie and Norman would probably scoff at the very idea of someone else choosing the things that surrounded them, that defined them.

His mother had routinely redecorated the house every other year, each version as cold and sterile as the last, each designed to impress rather than to comfort, none designed with a small boy in mind.

The Zwiebels' home radiated love, but Adam knew that love would be there no matter where they lived. Their affection for each other was a palpable thing and wrapped itself around whoever came into contact with it.

When he finished, Norman and Hattie thanked him profusely.

"If it wasn't for you, I don't know what we'd have done," Norman admitted. "When the doctor said Hattie couldn't come home, would have to go somewhere else because of the wheelchair . . ." He turned away and blew his nose.

"Neither do I," Hattie seconded, taking Adam's hand and squeezing it. Her voice faltered, and she sniffled. "I don't know what I'd have done if I couldn't have come back to my home. Thank you for making it happen."

Touched by the tears she didn't bother to wipe away, Adam bent to plant a kiss on Hattie's parchmentlike cheek. "I liked doing it," he said, and it was true.

"Don't you forget my Sunday dinner, you hear?" she reminded him as he gathered up his tools. "I'll make pot roast, new potatoes, and vegetables. Pumpkin pie for dessert."

"I'm counting on it." He shook hands with Norman and kissed Hattie once more.

Driving home, he smiled, remembering Hattie and Norman's gratitude for what, to him, had been a small thing. He was beginning to understand what Eden had tried to tell him: helping others firsthand gave meaning to life. Until he'd met her, he hadn't truly understood that.

His life had been busy, but, aside from his work, devoid of much meaning. The round of holiday parties he'd once enjoyed had long since turned flat, until he'd felt he was only going through the motions of pretending to have a good time.

It had taken Eden to turn his life around.

Adam didn't like the way Eden had been avoiding his gaze ever since he'd arrived that evening. She'd called him earlier, inviting him over for dessert and coffee. She had something to tell him. Of that, he was certain.

He was equally certain he wasn't going to like it.

After serving thick wedges of chocolate cake, she twisted a strand of hair between her fingers and began, hesitantly, to speak.

"Your mother called me today. She said she'd read about us in the paper but waited until the election was over to invite us to dinner. I thought you might be more comfortable if we got together here, so I invited them for Friday night at seven."

He was right. He didn't like it. "Uninvite them."

A silence settled between them.

Though she'd been prepared for his resistance to the idea, the flat tone of the command, the coldness in his eyes, frightened her. His voice was quiet. Too quiet. She'd have felt better if he'd yelled or something. Anything but this deadly calm.

"Adam, they sounded happy, really happy. Please do this. For me?"

He turned away. "No."

"Won't you even talk to them?"

"I haven't talked to my parents, except about the campaign, in years. I see no reason to start socializing with them now."

"There's every reason to start now. They're your parents. Doesn't that mean anything?"

He turned to her. The naked pain in his eyes had her taking his hand, but he shrugged her away.

"My parents' marriage isn't out of some storybook," he said. "My mother's idea of a family supper is a catered dinner for thirty of her most intimate friends. My father can't sit down for two minutes without a phone to his ear, checking on the market."

"Then this will be a change for them."

"You don't get it, do you? They don't *want* to change. They don't *want* to care. I spent the first eighteen years of my life trying to get them to do just that."

She heard the anguish in his voice, a pain he probably wasn't even aware of, and she ached for him. "They're your parents, Adam. They love you."

"They don't know the meaning of the word."

"Maybe it's time they learned."

"You can't teach love," he said in a flat voice. "Not to people like them." He shook his head, as though the words had left a foul taste in his mouth.

"They need you in their lives. They may not show it, but they miss you."

"They've never missed me. Do you know how I spent Easter, Thanksgiving, Christmas, before I was old enough to go to boarding school?" He didn't give her a chance to answer.

"With the maid. While they went off to Europe. Or St. Croix. Or New Zealand. Wherever was 'hot' that year. They never even bothered to ask if I wanted to go."

"And when you were older?"

"I stayed by myself." He gave her a hard look. "I liked it that way. I still like it that way." Anger pushed the words out.

"Give them a chance. People change."

"Not my parents."

"How do you know unless you talk to them?"

He leaned away from her, and she knew it was more than physical distance that he'd put between them. "Stay out of my life."

"I thought you wanted me to be a part of your life." She couldn't keep the hurt from her voice.

"I do."

"Just not this part. Is that it, Adam? I can be part of your life, but only the parts that are easy, convenient. The parts you decide to *allow* me into."

"That's not what I meant."

"Yes." She brushed his cheek with the back of one hand. "I'm afraid you did. I'm sorry."

"So am I."

He left after that. There was no good-bye kiss. No promise to call later. Nothing.

Eden had known all along that she and Adam were miles apart in their lifestyles, in their outlooks. Maybe in all ways.

It's for the best, she told herself.

The only problem was, she was having a hard time convincing her heart of that.

Chapter Nine

Adam couldn't sleep. The ticking of the clock on the nightstand reminded him that it was well past midnight. Moonlight lay across the hardwood floor in broken pieces. Symbolic, he reflected, of his heart.

He slapped back the sheet and blanket, battling a host of warring emotions. Eden had gone too far. Interfering with him and his parents had crossed a line.

After a miserable night, he rose early and dressed for his morning jog.

He ran as though trying to race the wind. In reality, his opponent was far more difficult to outrun. His thoughts churned with the fury of a whirlpool, swirling, spinning, spiraling out of control. A faint stitch in his side had him slowing down.

Eden. Eden. Eden. Her name pounded in his head in rhythm to the pounding of his feet on the pavement.

He slowed even more, his breath coming in harsh gasps, the cramp in his side now a raging pain. He couldn't outdistance his anger or his fear.

His anger would dissipate, he knew. Eden was only trying to help him come to terms with his parents. But his fear was escalating. Fear of facing the pain of his past.

He'd spent the better part of his adult life trying to forget it all. Could he now open that up, probe his feelings, and survive?

Overriding that was an even greater fear. Fear that Eden could never forgive him after the ugly words he'd hurled at her. Could he even forgive himself? Had he lost her forever with his stubbornness and fear?

The thought caused him to stop completely. He looked around, not recognizing his surroundings. How far had he run? Obviously not far enough to outdistance his thoughts. Leaning forward, he braced his hands on his knees, inhaling deeply.

He ignored the sharpening pain in his side as he headed home.

Five days ago he'd left Eden's in anger. He hadn't called since, and she hadn't either.

Five days.

One hundred and twenty hours.

Each had dragged by with a slowness that tried his patience and tested his resolve to stay away from his family and Eden's interference with it.

He'd gone through the motions of work, but his heart wasn't in it. His heart, he realized, belonged wherever Eden was.

Adam ultimately found Eden at the shelter's food pantry, stocking shelves. Content to simply watch her for a few moments, he leaned against a counter and absorbed the quiet intensity she brought to the task.

Streamers of sun worked their way through the ancient blinds, and dust motes danced wildly in the stripes of light. Sunlight landed on Eden's hair, creating a golden nimbus around her head.

He inhaled sharply at the picture she made.

She looked up at his intake of breath. "Adam." She pushed back a strand of hair that had fallen across her cheek. As he stepped over to her, she smelled like cinnamon, lemon polish, and everything good in life.

"I'm sorry." The words weren't as difficult to say as he'd feared.

"It's all right," she said, trailing her fingers along his cheek.

He caught them and brought them to his lips, kissing the tip of each finger in turn. "What did I ever do to deserve you?" he murmured.

"You love me. Just like I love you. That's all it takes."

He looked into the soft warmth of her eyes and knew she meant every word. Eden didn't ration out her love. She gave it fully, unconditionally.

He'd thought he understood that; now he realized he was only beginning to understand the full magnitude of what it meant to be loved by such a woman.

Before Eden had become part of his life, he'd assumed that everyone doled out love and approval as his parents had—with stingy hands and cold hearts. But Eden had introduced him to a new way of loving . . . and living.

He didn't want to go back to the old way, where love was

a commodity and approval was given or withheld, depending upon the whim of the other person. His thoughts took him full cycle. Back to his parents.

He searched Eden's face, wondering why he'd thought he had to hide that part of himself. Perhaps it was shame. Or pride. Or some twisted combination of the two. He chose his words carefully, needing to understand as much as to explain. Only then could he ask for her forgiveness.

"My parents and I have been strangers for as long as I can remember. I'd convinced myself I wanted it that way. But now . . . I'm not sure." The words caught in his throat, but he managed to get them out. "I'm afraid."

"Maybe they are too."

He started to deny it. His father, the power broker, afraid? The idea intrigued him. Adam couldn't imagine his father afraid of anything or anyone. Least of all his son.

And his mother? Adam tried to remember when he'd last seen his mother display any emotion at all.

"Your mother's really quite shy," Eden said, as if reading his mind.

He looked at her with undisguised skepticism. "You've talked with her once, maybe twice now? What makes you think she's shy?"

"I heard it in her voice. I could tell by her attitude."

Adam didn't doubt it. Eden could tell more about a person by just listening than most people could after a lengthy association. It was only part of what made her so special.

"If you gave her a chance, you might be surprised."

He thought about it. His mother was on the board of a half dozen charities. Invitations to her dinner parties were among the most sought after in the city.

"Give them a chance. That's all I'm asking. Give yourself a chance. People can and do change."

She was right. He was proof of it. But he hadn't done it on his own. It had taken Eden and a hard look at his life to turn him around. Maybe his parents needed the same kind of help. Maybe he was the one who could do it. Maybe . . .

A smile rested on his lips. Eden was doing it again. Getting him to believe in miracles.

"I tried to stay away," he said as he helped her finish stocking and lock up the food pantry.

"I know. I missed you."

"Good." He couldn't quite keep the satisfaction from his voice.

"What about dinner with your parents?"

"If it means so much to you, I'll do it." He heard his words as if from a distance and hoped he wouldn't live to regret them.

"Thank you."

The smile in her voice did funny things to his heart, and he realized he'd do anything to keep her happy.

"We have something special between us. You feel it, don't you?" she murmured.

"Yes. Only . . . I'm afraid."

"Don't be. Just let it happen."

Adam sealed their new beginning with a kiss, a kiss that promised all the things he couldn't say. Yet. Reluctantly, he released her.

"Where are we heading?" she asked him.

"I don't know. But I think it's worth finding out. Don't you?"

"Yes. I do."

Outside, they braced themselves against the wind. Ocher, saffron, and amber leaves caught the sun and held it, creating a glittering mist of gold as they danced in the stiff wind.

Adam tucked her arm under his, holding her close beside him.

"Okay if I call tonight?" he asked when they reached her car.

"I'd like that."

Adam walked back to where he'd left his car, his step lighter than it had been in a week.

Because of Eden.

The night of their dinner with his parents arrived more quickly than Adam would have wished.

Eden greeted the elder Forsythes with the same casual grace she did the people at the shelter. She didn't have one set of manners for the rich and pampered of the world and another for those who took their meals at a soup kitchen.

Adam noticed the slight flush in his father's cheeks. He had never known Matthew Forsythe to be embarrassed or made uneasy by anything. He caught Eden watching him and felt his own cheeks turn warm under her gaze.

He was doing this for her, he reminded himself, as she settled everyone in the living room with wine and hors d'oeuvres. There was no law saying he had to like his parents; all he had to do was get through the evening. He could do that much.

When Eden mentioned over dinner that the hospital's ladies' auxiliary was holding a Christmas bazaar to raise money for the shelter and pantry, his mother opened up with, "How much do you hope to make?"

"A couple of thousand dollars, if we're lucky. That would feed a lot of people."

"Oh, we can do better than that," Kitty said with a confident smile.

" 'We'?" Eden echoed gently.

For the first time that Adam could remember, his mother looked unsure of herself. "I'd like to help. If you'll let me."

Adam stared, openmouthed, until Eden gently kicked him under the table. He'd never known his mother to offer her assistance to any cause that wasn't approved by the social lions of Eagleton.

But then, he shouldn't have been surprised. He already knew the magic Eden cast on those who fell under her spell. He sat back to watch the miracle take place.

"I'd like that, Mrs. Forsythe," Eden said softly. "We could use someone with your experience."

A soft blush smudged his mother's cheeks. "Please, dear, call me Kitty."

They spent the rest of the evening discussing various fundraising ideas. Adam listened in amazement as his mother offered Eden some surprisingly sharp insights.

Kitty Forsythe snapped her fingers. "I know. We'll hold an auction. I'll ask all my friends to contribute and then invite them to attend. People love to think they're getting a bargain." She smiled conspiratorially. "I have a lot of favors to call in. I've just been waiting for the right occasion.

"I'll make some calls tonight," she promised, patting Eden's hand. "Don't you worry. If there's one thing I know how to do, it's raise money."

By the end of the evening, Adam had mellowed enough

to start seeing his parents in a new way, and everyone was talking and laughing easily together.

Matthew Forsythe gave Eden a bemused look. "You must be a magician, young lady," he said. "You've got Adam and us acting like a family for the first time in years."

It was true. Whatever Eden had done had softened the hard edge Adam's father had always worn like a suit of armor. To his knowledge, his father rarely smiled, much less laughed. And he'd never seen his mother so engaged or engaging either. With Eden, she actually giggled!

Adam sipped his glass of wine. Eden had accomplished in one evening what neither he nor his parents had been able to in years.

"And I thank heaven for it," his mother said, reaching up to brush her lips against Adam's cheek as she and his father prepared to leave.

Adam felt as if he'd wandered into another dimension. He couldn't remember the last time his mother had kissed him. Sometime around his eighth birthday, he thought.

His mother and father would never win any awards as parents of the year, but he was beginning to see them as decent people with their own brand of affection and caring to offer. It was up to him to find a way to accept it—and them.

The Forsythes had barely said good night when Eden turned and threw her arms around Adam. "Thank you." She kissed him lightly. With sweetness. With promise.

Automatically, his arms closed around her. "No, thank *you.*"

"Your mother was great," Eden said. "I should ask her to chair the shelter's annual food drive."

Adam didn't have to pretend enthusiasm for the idea this

time. He'd seen the sparkle in his mother's eyes when Eden welcomed her help. Eden was doing it again—working her own brand of sorcery.

He curled his hands over her shoulders but put enough distance between them so that he could see her face. His father was right about Eden's being a magician, he reflected. How else could he explain what had transpired this evening?

"How do you do it?" He saw the genuine bewilderment in her eyes. She had no idea how much she'd accomplished.

"Do what?"

"Never mind," he said, drawing her to him once more. For years, he'd struggled to find common ground with his parents. Eventually he'd given up. But all it had taken was one evening with Eden to have their acting like a family.

It was always Eden.

The many layers of feeling this woman generated in him took on even more texture. Respect, admiration, tenderness, and love. Always love.

"Your parents just need to learn how to show their love," she said. "We can teach them."

There was no better teacher on earth, he thought.

Linking her hands around his neck, she pulled his head down until their lips brushed, then deepened in a kiss so sweet that it squeezed his heart.

When she spoke his name, the tenderness shattered him.

"It's never been like this," he murmured. "Never."

"I know." Her words were as soft as the lips he'd so recently touched.

"How did I ever survive without you?"

"Who said you did?"

He stroked the hair that lay like silk around her shoulders before brushing it aside to press a kiss to the sweet curve of her neck. She turned in his arms so that her lips met his again.

"You're so beautiful," he murmured. He kissed her again, letting his lips linger on hers as he savored the wonder that she belonged to him.

Something in her eyes made him want to promise her everything.

"I love you," he whispered against her hair.

"I know. Just like I love you."

It was that simple. And that complicated. *Love.* A four-letter word that had changed his life. That, and a very special woman. He started to tell her just that, then stopped himself.

He'd never convince her that it was her magic that sparked so much love in others. He did the next best thing. He raised their linked hands and brushed his lips over her knuckles.

"The food pantry needs more funds," Adam said, warming to his subject at his first meeting as a council member. "With the unemployment rate on the rise, more and more people need assistance. The pantry and shelters can't operate without money."

"Adam, Adam." Harry Roberts smiled genially, though there was not a drop of humor in his voice. "We'd all like to be able to budget more money for the poor. I think I speak for everyone here when I say we all feel sorry for those people." He looked around the oval table at the other members of the council and was rewarded with a chorus of murmured assents.

"But money's tight. I don't have to tell you that. You understand the economics of the situation."

Adam knew the realities only too well, even as he resented Harry's patronizing tone. He'd seen the desperate need, felt it, tasted it. Harsh realities, like a mother going without food so that her child could eat. The reality of not enough food and too many people in need.

He checked the angry words that threatened to escape his lips. He'd only manage to antagonize Harry, one of his chief supporters, and other council members as well.

He had to try reason one more time. "If you visit the shelter and pantry, you'll see what I mean."

Harry narrowed his eyes. "You're sounding like that doctor you brought to my home. Such emotion is all well and fine for someone like that. But you've got to maintain some objectivity here."

"While we're being 'objective,' there are people going hungry." Despite his best efforts, Adam's anger seeped through. "Children who have nothing to eat."

"This being your first time and all on the council, Adam, it might be wise if you sat back and listened," Harry said. His voice was mild, but his eyes were hard. "You might pick up some pointers."

Adam caught the looks being exchanged. If he weren't careful, he'd destroy any chance he had of making a difference in people's lives. He'd bide his time, but he didn't intend to remain silent forever. He had vowed to make a difference for his city, for his people. For Eden.

He listened as the council discussed other issues on the agenda. Only when the meeting broke up did Harry turn to him.

"You're bright, Adam. Too bright to be making enemies your first day." The warning was unmistakable.

"Sorry," Adam said briefly.

Harry smiled. "No problem. You'll learn the ropes soon enough."

Adam had a feeling he might be learning more than he ever wanted to. He'd already learned an important lesson today. If he wanted the council to do something, he had to present it in a way they understood. And that meant appealing to their business sense.

He gathered up his papers and headed to the bank of elevators on the fourth floor of city hall. He had some calls to make.

Chapter Ten

Adam arrived at Eden's house at eight, holding a flat of winter pansies. When he'd seen them in an outdoor market, he knew he had to get them. Their color, sunshine-bright and free from artifice, reminded him of Eden.

When she opened the door, he handed them to her.

"What's the occasion?"

"They're a no-occasion present."

"The best kind," she said, smiling.

He knew she was waiting for him to kiss her, and he complied. The quick peck on her cheek drew a surprised look from her, but she didn't comment.

She laced her fingers around his neck to draw him closer for a real kiss. "I have wonderful news," she said when she drew away. "We found it. The perfect piece of property. Just outside of town. It's perfect, absolutely perfect. Well, almost. It's—"

"Hold on. Slow down, and take a deep breath. It's not going anywhere, is it?"

She frowned, the gesture puckering her lips. "That's the

part we're not sure about. Some other organization has their eye on it, so we have to act fast. The city has to approve it, of course. Then we have to make our bid. And then—"

Adam kissed her. "And then you have to let me take you out to dinner to celebrate."

"No time. There's too much to do."

He kissed her again. "We'll make time. For everything. Now tell me all about it."

He listened while Eden filled him in on the details of the proposed property for the community garden. When she told him its location, he frowned. Something niggled at the back of his mind until it focused. Zoning laws. He struggled to remember what they were for the location in question.

His conscience stirred restlessly.

"Is something wrong?" she asked.

He wouldn't brood on it. Not when a tiny line had dug its way between Eden's eyebrows. Maybe he was wrong. He prayed so.

He'd research the property. If the report came up negative, there'd be time enough to break the bad news to her later.

Coward.

He appeased his conscience with the reminder that he didn't know for certain that the property would be unsuitable. He had only his suspicions.

Eden kept talking, oblivious to his growing concern. That was the way he wanted it for now. If his fears were groundless, there'd be no problem. If, however, they weren't . . .

He let the thought go unfinished, unwilling to pursue it at the moment.

Eden's voice broke into his thoughts. "You'll back us, won't you?"

He took his time in answering, choosing his words carefully. "If the research shows the property is right for Grow a Garden, I'll support it with everything I have."

Apparently she didn't hear the reservation in his voice, for she threw her arms around his neck. "You care. You really care."

Tell her about your doubts about the location. She'll understand.

Why spoil her excitement until you know for sure that the location isn't right?

It'll be easier in the long run if you tell her about your doubts now.

Coward.

The inner dialogue between his heart and his mind played over and over until he wasn't sure of anything. The only thing he knew was, he couldn't stand to ever lose Eden. Over this or anything else.

When she lifted her lips to his once more, he kissed her. As his lips met hers, he shelved his doubts.

Eden had worked too hard to make her dream come true. He wouldn't—he *couldn't*—be the one to destroy it.

He loved her too much.

Hours spent at the office were thieves slipping past, stealing time Adam might otherwise spend with Eden. Her excitement over the proposed community garden site grew every day, along with his anxiety as the council's city planner investigated it.

Harry Roberts stuck his head into Adam's office. "Adam, got a minute?"

"Sure. Come on in."

Inwardly, Adam groaned. The last thing he wanted was another bit of "friendly advice" from Harry on "learning the ropes." Harry's advice usually consisted of the importance of being a team player, translated: *don't make waves.*

"It's this proposal for the site for that garden that do-gooder girlfriend of yours is pushing," Harry said, tossing a file onto Adam's desk.

Adam ignored the reference to Eden. Harry would never understand anyone who devoted herself to helping others. "What about it?"

"It's not going to work."

"Why not?"

"Look at the planner's report, and tell me what you think."

Adam scanned the file. Whatever he might think of Harry, he couldn't fault the concise, detailed report in front of him. Proximity to public transportation, housing, and everything else made the site Eden's group proposed a desperate choice, just as Adam had feared.

More than that, the current zoning laws did prohibit any kind of structure there. Eden's group wanted to build a second food pantry and shelter in conjunction with the garden.

"Well?" Harry demanded.

Adam loosened his tie and undid the top button of his shirt. It had already been a long day. It promised to get longer. "I see what you mean."

"We decided to go ahead with the vote today. You'll be there?"

"Yeah, I'll be there."

Harry hesitated, looking unsure of himself for the first time. "You still seeing Dr. Hathaway?"

Adam gave a brief nod.

"She feels pretty strongly about the land for the community garden, doesn't she?"

"She's worked toward it for a long time," he said evenly.

"Might make it rough on you."

"If you're asking if that will affect how I do my job, then you don't know me very well." Adam didn't bother to disguise the coolness in his tone.

"Didn't mean to ruffle your feathers," Harry said with a casualness that mocked Adam's worry. "I know you'll do the right thing." He smirked, the closest to a smile he ever got.

Adam stayed in his office until the last moment before the vote was taken, trying to find a way of making the proposed site work for the community garden. But the facts hadn't changed, no matter how much he might want them to. In the end, he did what was necessary and voted against the site.

He stepped out of city hall, knowing he'd done the only thing he could. But how did he tell Eden that he'd voted against something for which she'd worked so hard?

Admit it, Forsythe. You're a coward. A first-class coward who's afraid to face the woman you love.

The drive to Eden's house took less time than he'd hoped, and still he was exhausted. From the day. From the tension. From the thoughts circling like vultures in his mind as he prepared to face what he had to do.

"I didn't expect you tonight," she said as she let him inside. She laced her arms around his neck and lifted her face for a kiss.

Adam gently freed himself from her embrace and started to pace. He needed distance between them in order to say what he had to.

"Is something wrong?"

"The council voted today on the land."

"Great. That means we can start moving forward on the project even sooner than we'd hoped. We'll push through the paperwork. We already have a promise from a major supplier to donate seeds, topsoil—all the things we need to get started. I'm working with a master gardener right now. He's donating his services." She hugged herself and twirled around. "Finally, it's all coming together."

Adam's breath caught as she turned to him. She was beautiful, happiness shimmering in her eyes. But he knew that that happiness was fragile, tenuous. In that instant, he hated himself for what he was about to say.

"Eden, the council voted against the site." The agony of what he was saying, what it would do to Eden, plunged into his soul.

"I . . . I don't understand."

He saw the confusion in her face, the beginnings of pain replacing the happiness that had been there only seconds before. It was his fault. If he'd told her about his fears in the beginning, he might have saved her a world of disappointment.

"Why did they vote against it? I thought you said it would pass."

"I said I thought it had a good chance, provided the planner's reports came back favorable."

"They didn't?"

He sighed heavily. "No. They showed—"

"Who voted against it?"

A muscle worked at his temple. "Does it matter?"

Now it was her turn to pace. "Roberts, for sure. And probably Whitcomb and Stanley. Didn't you say they're golf buddies?"

"They play golf together," he agreed. "But that's not why the vote turned out the way it did." He hesitated, trying to find the right words. "I'm sorry," he began, wincing at his inadequacy.

"It's not your fault," she said, crossing the room to wrap her arms around his waist. "I know you did your best. If only there were more on the city council like you, we'd have our garden." She signed wearily. "Now we just have to start over."

Guilt dug its teeth deeper. Truth pulled at him, the burden of full accountability. Adam pulled back, looked into her trusting eyes, and knew he couldn't let a lie stand between them, even an unspoken one. "I voted against it too."

She didn't speak, only stared at him. When the words came, they were laced with bewilderment and pain. "I don't believe it! You said you believed in what we were doing. You want the garden as much as I do. I know you do!"

"I did. I do. But—"

"But what?" Her breathing had slowed, a deliberate sound that told of her suffering more than words.

"The research showed—"

"I don't care what the research showed!" Her angry, accusing tone stabbed the air. "I only care why you voted against us! Why, Adam? Why?" She glared at him, eyes burning with reproach.

He didn't entirely blame her. "If you'll let me explain—"

"Explain what? Explain why you voted against a project that could help so many people? Explain why you voted against a way to help feed hungry children? Explain why you voted against everything I believe in?" Fury gathered on her face.

Adam took a deep breath, hearing the anguish in her voice and knowing he'd helped put it there. "You might not believe this, but I do still want to help you and your group. The site—"

"You're right. I don't believe it." Disdain coated her voice. Beneath that, though, was misery.

He flinched at the pain in her eyes, deeply injured that she could think so little of him.

"You know how I feel about you," he said in a low voice, putting aside, for the moment, the rational reasons for finding another site. "I love you."

Her voice fell to a whisper. "Do you?" She held her head high, but her eyes were moist, and he felt certain she was keeping the tears at bay by sheer force of will.

The thought that he had hurt her wounded him more than he had even thought possible, far more than the pain her words had caused. She was lashing out in her own pain and anger.

"You know I do. I thought you felt the same," he said quietly.

She turned away.

He grabbed her and spun her around, forcing her to look at him. "I love you. I've never said those words to another woman." And he never would. He knew that as surely as he knew anything.

"How can you say you love me and then try to destroy

everything I believe in?" She put a hand to her mouth, visibly struggling for self-control. "Do you know what losing that piece of land means? It means we have to start all over from scratch.

"Even if we do find something in the next couple of months, we'll have to wade through the city bureaucracy and the paperwork you suits love to throw at nonprofit groups. That means we'll lose the spring planting season. That means we wait another whole year. Another year while children go hungry. Can you live with that?" She poked a finger at his chest. "I can't."

He ignored the reference to him as a "suit." "Eden, what I feel for you has nothing to do with the garden. And, for the record, I didn't vote against Grow a Garden. I voted against the *location*." He took a deep breath, trying to check the anger that threatened to spill over. If he gave way to it now, they were both lost. "I voted against an inappropriate piece of property, not you." *Never you.*

"That 'inappropriate piece of property' is what I've spent the last six months of my life working for." The quaver in her voice clearly came as much from a sense of betrayal as anger.

"It can't possibly be the only land available. We'll find a different site, a better one—"

"There isn't one," she said, the grief in her voice tearing his heart to shreds. "Don't you think we searched for something better? Something that would give us everything we wanted? This was the best we could come up with."

"I'll help you. I'll spend every minute I can spare looking for the right property. If we work together, we can—"

"Thanks but no thanks. We've had more than enough of your kind of 'help.' We can't afford any more." Her fists, he noted, were clenched at her sides. He almost wished she would use them on him. They'd hurt less than seeing the pain in her eyes did.

He wanted to haul her into his arms and kiss away the bitterness he read in her gaze. Tears now streamed down her cheeks like silver ribbons. He reached out, intending to wipe them away, but she brushed his hand away.

"Don't touch me." The sadness on her face destroyed him.

"It wasn't the right place," he said in an even tone. "If you looked at our research, you'd see that for yourself."

Her gaze raked him with cold contempt. "What I *see* is another *politician,*" she hissed in the anger that was driving her so irrationally. The words stung, but he tried again. "Maybe if your Grow a Garden had checked out the property more thoroughly, you'd have seen that the location and the zoning laws would never let you do what you wanted."

She gazed at him with what looked like pure contempt. "Good-bye, Adam."

He started toward her, but she stopped him with only that look. Knowing she needed time to sort through her own emotions, her own failure, and to grieve the indefinite postponement of her fondest dream, he sadly let himself out.

Icy rain pummeled him as he walked to his car, and he turned up his collar against the cold. He was grateful for the sleet as he drove home. Negotiating the miserably slick roads kept his pain at bay.

At home, he started toward the phone, then stopped. He'd give her time. As much as she needed. He'd stay away. As long as she needed him to. But not forever, he promised himself. Not forever.

With slow, even breaths, he tried to calm his heart. Even then, it still ached.

"It's not over, sweetheart," he said aloud. "Not by a long shot."

When Eden awakened in the morning, it took a few seconds to remember. Then it hit her.

Adam.

The garden site.

Both were gone and, along with them, her dream. Grief rolled over her, numbed her. She shook off her lethargy and forced herself to climb out of bed. She padded into the bathroom, looked in the mirror, and wanted to cry. Pale cheeks, red-rimmed eyes, and matted hair gave mute evidence of her miserable night.

She slid down to the floor, pulled her knees up to her chest, and rested her chin on them. Tears filled her eyes. Her throat burned with the effort to hold them back.

The sobs wanted to leap out of her throat, but she feared if she gave in to them, she would never stop. And wasn't that pitiful? A grown woman afraid to cry because she didn't know if she could ever stop.

She was still trying to come to grips with what had happened. Part of it seemed surreal, as if it had happened to someone else and she was merely a bystander, watching a play.

But the pain in her heart was real. Very real.

She could barely summon enough energy to eat the breakfast she forced herself to make. It tasted as flat as she felt.

Resolutely, she took one bite at a time. Somehow she would have to go on. One day at a time.

The morning had dawned gray and dreary, the air heavy, as though with her tears. Thin rain fell not so much in drops as in drizzle. Tattered clouds cast the day into perpetual gloom.

She made herself go through the motions of cleaning up and preparing to face the day.

How could I have been so wrong? Dear heaven, how could I have been so wrong?

The question plagued her, undermining her confidence, until she longed to huddle in a miserable heap. There was plenty to do that she didn't feel up to doing. She had a grant to write, a mother-and-tot group to teach, a speech to prepare for an upcoming fund-raiser.

The rain continued, slow and thin, a mirror to the grayness that blanketed her heart.

The day set the pattern for those to come. Eden pushed her way through them by force of will. And if, in the privacy of her home, she gave way to the heartache that was never far away, no one would have to know.

She thought about the past, the efficiency with which she had run her life. She had always known where she was going, what she needed to do, and how she would accomplish it. She was petite, but that knowledge had always added metaphorical inches to her height.

Now her certainty seemed to be at an all-time low, making her feel small, inadequate, and powerless.

When a week passed, Eden acknowledged that, despite everything, she still loved Adam, would always love him.

She'd always believed that love was enough to endure any obstacle.

She'd been wrong.

She hadn't been sleeping. Memories of the last time she'd seen Adam haunted her nights, making sleep impossible. They invaded the daylight hours as well, until she was no longer sure which was which.

All she wanted to do was push thoughts of him out of her mind, strip her memory of any images of him.

Some days were better than others. She'd added more hours at the pantry, taken on yet more volunteer work, determined to fill the hours until she was too tired to think. Or to feel. But her strategy didn't work. She was tired, all right, close to exhaustion, but it didn't make sleep come any more easily.

The pain mercifully blunted to a dull ache that merely throbbed in her chest. It didn't rip her apart, as she'd feared it might. Instead, it had settled in her heart with depressing heaviness.

She wanted to cry, but the tears would no longer come, no matter how she wished they would. Tears might provide some small release from the pain lodged in her heart. She felt her throat fill and burn.

Perhaps, she reflected, there was a grief so intense that nothing could ease it.

She felt as though large parts of herself had been ripped away, like a jigsaw puzzle missing so many pieces that only a part of the picture could be put together.

Adam had filled the empty places in her life, places she hadn't even known existed . . . until he'd shown her. A soft warmth stole over her as she remembered the tenderness of his kisses.

Her spirits lifted for a moment as she remembered that she had promised to substitute for a friend coaching the girls' basketball team of a local church. Their game was that night.

Eden arrived at the gymnasium in the community center with five minutes to spare before the game.

"Hey, Doc Hathaway, over here!" one of the girls called.

Eden jogged over to where her team huddled. After a brief pep talk, she gave each of the girls a high five and said a silent prayer that she was up to the job.

Whoever said that coaching a girls' basketball team would be easy obviously didn't know what he was talking about, she thought thirty minutes later.

Getting too close to a girl while she was outlining a play resulted in an elbow to Eden's eye.

"Sorry, coach," the girl said.

"No problem."

Eden gingerly touched her left eye and struggled to keep her right eye focused on the game. She raced up and down the court, trying to keep up with six teenage girls, all of whom exuded an energy she couldn't hope to match. Obviously, she was more out of shape than she'd realized.

An accidental kick to her shin by a member of the opposing team had her clutching her leg while she squinted through her uninjured eye. She managed to smile around a grimace of pain and reminded herself that the game was nearly over.

When one of her girls scored another two points, bringing the final score to 52 versus 50, the team screamed, rallying around her.

Eden found herself as excited as the girls and treated them to hamburgers and fries at a fast-food place.

On an impulse, she stopped at Hattie and Norman's place on her way home. They could always cheer her up, and she desperately needed that right now, desperately needed to escape the snare of her lonely thoughts. Just the prospect of being around them and witnessing their love for each other lifted her spirits.

As she started to back her ancient car into the one remaining parking space on the street, she noticed a car parked in front of their house. Adam's car.

She paused. At the same moment, a dead leaf fell onto the hood of her car—dull, drab, discouraging, a perfect match to her mood.

Her heart hammered against her ribs. She ached to see Adam yet shied away from it, remembering the angry, irrational words she'd tossed at him the last time they'd been together. The heat of her anger had long since passed, but all her misgivings had now frozen into a glacier around her heart.

She pulled away from the curb and drove home, swiping at the moisture that had gathered in the corners of her eyes. She blinked at the sudden glare of wintry sun and managed to convince herself that her tears were the result of that. A great depression grew inside her.

It didn't surprise her that Adam was visiting the Zwiebels. He'd told her he felt more at home there than he ever had in the house where he'd been raised. What surprised her was the sense of being excluded she now felt.

Angrily, she reminded herself that she had no right to feel left out. Hattie and Norman were certainly entitled to entertain anyone they chose. So why did she feel like crying?

Because, even knowing what she did, she couldn't help loving Adam. She had no one to blame but herself. She'd known what she was risking when she became involved with him. She just hadn't known how much it was going to hurt. Her heart squeezed in anguish.

Once at home, she finally cried. When her sobs subsided into hiccups, she walked to the mirror and looked at herself. Red-rimmed eyes stared back at her. Okay, she'd had her cry. Now it was time to get on with her life.

More tired than she'd ever been, she dropped onto the sofa and tried not to feel. If she could turn off her feelings, then maybe she could survive the night.

She didn't dare think beyond that.

Adam was still the man she loved.

The hours stumbled over one another, rushing to pile up into days until it was almost Christmas Eve. Eden welcomed the extra demands of the holiday season; they kept her from thinking—and feeling—too much. Despite the extra demands, she felt brutally alone.

She still had to search for a new garden site. She certainly had other obligations, but she couldn't shake the depression that hovered over her like a dingy cloud. Suddenly everything seemed impossible.

Her eyes burned dryly from sleeplessness. What had once been joys now became duties.

That realization left a bitter taste in her mouth. When

had she become so selfish that she resented what she had once loved?

For bits and pieces of time, she'd become so absorbed in what she was doing that the ache in her heart had diminished a fraction.

But Adam was never far from her thoughts. *Adam.* Despite her best efforts to banish his face from her memory, his name lingered around the edges of her mind. The happiness she'd shared with him now came back to mock her, to taunt her with memories. Odd how happiness could seem to get a solid grip on you, then tear your heart out when it left.

She found herself asking the question that had plagued humanity from almost the beginning of time: was it truly better to have loved and lost than never to have loved at all? She honestly didn't know.

The torment of wanting things she couldn't have was crushing. Sometimes it was better to push them from her mind and pretend they just didn't exist. She shoved aside the drapes and looked out the window. The world had turned to rock candy, with glassy ice coating every shrub and tree.

When she stepped outside, with dawn barely a bruise on the horizon, she winced. The air was gray and heavy, an echo of her heart. The grass was hard and crunchy, a thick, stiff carpet. Her feet kicked up shards of snow as she walked across the lawn to her car. She barely registered the freezing spray.

She mentally catalogued her upcoming day, making sure every minute was filled. She couldn't allow time to think, to feel, to remember. Any pleasure she might have experienced in holiday traditions and activities was smeared by her loss of Adam.

Catching a glimpse of her future, a future without Adam, she felt a deep inner pang. Still, the food pantry needed supplies. Interest in her mother-tot nutrition group had grown so much that she'd started a second class. Another cold spell had pushed more people off the streets and into the shelter.

Unfortunately, supplies hadn't kept up with the influx of people. Eden used the money she'd been saving to have her house painted in the spring to purchase groceries.

"You shouldn't have done it," Richard said, hefting three large boxes of staples from her car. "But we need it too much for me to refuse."

She picked up two smaller boxes and followed him into the shelter. "I wish it were more."

"So do I," he said frankly. "But everything's appreciated."

They made several more trips until the car was empty.

Richard set the last of the boxes on the kitchen counter and turned to her. "Your friend came by yesterday."

Her heart stilled. "Adam?"

"Yeah. Brought by some coats. Said they were just lying around, and he didn't need them. Thing was, they still had the tags on them. I figure he went out and bought them and then was too embarrassed to admit it. Funny kind of guy."

"Yeah. Funny." She didn't want to feel gratitude toward Adam. A nasty knot coiled in her stomach. She wished— oh, how she wished—it would vanish.

Yet his unexpected kindness toward the people who made their home in the shelter was unbearably touching. It wrenched her, when she didn't want to be wrenched.

A terrible yearning twisted through her. She pushed it away with a force of will she hadn't known she possessed.

"We'd better get this stuff put away." Richard started unpacking the boxes. "You and Adam must have been on the same wavelength. He brought in a couple of sacks of food along with the coats."

That stopped her for a moment. She resumed filling the cabinets with the foodstuffs.

"Hey, do you really want to put those in there?" Richard asked.

"What?" Eden looked down at the bags of lettuce and spinach in her hands. "Sorry. I guess my mind was somewhere else."

Richard smiled. "I'd say that was a fair guess."

After they finished the job, she stayed, helping prepare the noonday meal. When they'd served the shelter's residents, she gave a tired sigh and rolled back her sleeves, preparing to wash dishes.

She turned on the water and squirted detergent into the sink. Memories of Adam helping her clean up after the hospital potluck and wash dishes at home assailed her.

Unbidden, a smile came. He'd been so kind to the ladies of the auxiliary. She thought of how he'd taken the time to compliment each woman on her special contribution to the meal. He'd been extremely kind and generous to Hattie and Norman as well, fixing up their house so that Hattie could return home.

He'd always been kind to her too. She remembered the way he'd come looking for her when she'd been delivering sandwiches and coffee to street people. Other memories crowded upon those, and reluctantly she recalled the way he had held her, as though she were something infinitely precious, the way he'd kissed her with heartbreaking tenderness.

"Why don't you go on home?" Richard suggested. "You look beat."

She knew she looked worse than that. "Trying to get rid of me already? Who're you going to find who loves to wash dishes as much as I do?" she joked, but her voice sounded as hollow as she felt.

Richard didn't respond to her teasing but took her hands from the sudsy water and handed her a towel. "I'm worried about you, kid. You've been running yourself ragged for the last two weeks, trying to be everywhere at once. Here. At the Zwiebels'. Teaching classes. Coaching basketball games."

Her eyes burned with sleeplessness, but she shrugged her exhaustion away. "There's a lot to be done."

"You can't do everything yourself." He gave her a long, probing look. "When are you going to slow down?"

"I can't."

"That's what I was afraid of. It's him, isn't it? Adam Forsythe."

She thought about denying it but knew she couldn't. "How did you know?"

"I saw the way you looked at him. What's more, I saw the way he looked at you. The man loves you."

Direct hit. It arrowed straight to her heart. Her breath jerked, forcing her to take a gulp of air or sob. "You're wrong."

"Am I?" With the ease of long friendship, he pulled her into a hug.

She leaned into his shoulder.

"How do you feel about him?"

She waited, hoping the words wouldn't come. She didn't want them to be true, believed they couldn't be true, but knew they were. Her heart empty, she swallowed hard to keep that void from echoing in her voice. "I love him."

For a few brief weeks, she'd dreamed of making a home, a family, with Adam. There'd be children, a big sloppy dog, a couple of bikes in the driveway.

But that dream was lost now, and like most lost dreams, it was hard to bear. She longed for Adam's touch. Her arms ached for the sweet weight of his baby to fill them.

"Then tell him."

"It's not that simple."

"No? Why not?"

She closed her eyes and steadied herself. "Adam voted against Grow a Garden, Grow a Child." She heard the husky, ruined voice and marveled that it was hers.

"I know."

"You know? How?"

"Did you think a city council vote was going to remain a secret? But didn't he tell you *why* he voted against it?"

She started to shake her head before remembering that Adam *had* tried to explain his reasons. She'd refused to listen. "He said something about the location being all wrong."

"He was right."

She turned to stare at Richard in astonishment. "It was the best site we could find."

"That doesn't mean it was right," Richard said in a calm way, and he began to dry the dishes Eden had washed. "You know it was cut off from public transportation, schools—everything our people need. And we couldn't have built a shelter or pantry."

"Adam said something like that."

"You didn't believe him?"

She thought about it. "No, I guess not. I knew the location's drawbacks, but I wanted the garden so much." Had she let her passion for the project, the children she so much wanted to help, blind her to the truth?

"We all do. But it won't do any good if it's not in the right place to help the people who need it most."

Adam had said the same thing, she remembered. He'd said a lot of things, but she'd been too hurt, too irrationally angry, to listen.

"Why is it that I feel like the guilty party?" she asked, more of herself than of Richard. "Adam's the one who voted against the site, but I feel guilty. It doesn't make sense."

"Doesn't it?"

She looked up at Richard in hurt and bewilderment. He had been her friend for years, and now he was siding with Adam.

"You think I'm wrong?" She hated the stiffness in her voice.

"I think that sometimes, when you're passionate about something, you lead with your heart instead of your head. That works some of the time but not always."

Her mouth curved slightly as she acknowledged the truth of Richard's words.

"Hey," he said with an awkward pat to her shoulder. "That's not a bad way to live, mind you. Your heart's as big as the sky. Just don't let it keep you from seeing what's real."

"I need to do some thinking." She felt a tear arrive without warning.

Richard reached out to wipe it away.

Eden returned home, put on a CD of holiday music, and curled up on the sofa. Tomorrow she would put in extra time at the shelter. There was always plenty there to occupy her time, her attention, her energy.

Tonight was for Christmas carols and quiet thoughts.

She thought about Richard's words far into the night. Had she been too quick to condemn Adam without hearing him out? Had she worked so long toward her goal that she'd blinded herself to everything and everyone else? She cringed when she thought of her self-righteousness.

The questions chipped away at her until she no longer knew what was right. This time she didn't try to stop her thoughts from circling back to Adam. Missing him was like feeling a phantom limb. Her memories of him were as vivid as if she were experiencing his love right now.

She knew she loved him. Still. Always.

With that admission, she felt some of the pain scorching her heart ease.

Was it too late for them?

Chapter Eleven

Adam had never felt so alone. He understood that, because of losing Eden, who had made him feel not alone for the first time, he'd never experience that feeling again. How could he live without that, without her?

He'd hoped that "giving her space" would bring her to the same conclusion—that they needed each other—but she had remained aloof, kept her distance. Except in his mind. She was always there, skirting the edges of his thoughts. He missed her more than he'd thought possible, and an emptiness yawned inside of him.

"Adam, we need your input," Harry said, more than a note of censure in his voice.

Guiltily, Adam looked up from where he'd been doodling on a printed agenda for the meeting. He was remembering the pain he'd put onto Eden's face their last night together. He'd stayed away from her since then, for both their sakes. He'd promised himself he wouldn't try to see her until he'd found a way out of the mess his actions had created.

With an effort, he shook himself out of the blue funk he'd fallen into. "Sorry, Harry. You were saying?"

Someone chuckled. "What's the matter, Adam? Woman trouble?"

"Why don't we stick to business?" Adam returned evenly. "What's up?"

"There's an abandoned warehouse on the corner of Cherry and Madison," Harry said. "We've got to make a decision on it. Developers want it demolished and the land zoned for residential use. Right now, the city owns it. Default on back taxes."

Adam studied the report Harry placed in front of him. He scanned the pages with little interest until he noticed the location. Something clicked in his brain, a breath of an idea that inched its way through the fog he'd been operating under for the past weeks.

"You say the city owns it?" he asked slowly.

"Yeah. Right now it's a white elephant. Not to mention an eyesore."

"I might have an idea," Adam said.

"Well, let's have it." Harry folded his arms across his chest.

"Can you give me a day or two? I want to do some checking before I stick my neck out."

"Sure. Only don't take any longer than that. We've got to make a decision on this and get back to the developers. I'm favoring going along with them. New housing would give us an increased tax base."

Adam tried to focus on the remaining items on the agenda for the rest of the meeting, but his mind kept drifting back to the report on the warehouse and the surrounding land. It was crazy, he told himself. Certifiably crazy.

There'd be all sorts of obstacles, including complaints from the developers who wanted to turn the land into a subdivision of upscale houses.

But his step was light as he left the meeting.

That night, Adam shoved away the papers he'd been studying and stretched. He'd spent the afternoon at city hall poring over building permits, regulations, and zoning laws. After grabbing a hamburger on the way home, he'd eaten while hunched over a sheaf of reports on the warehouse. But he had what he wanted.

He'd also paid a visit to the property, his excitement growing with every minute. The land would need work, the warehouse would need more, but it could work.

It could work.

The empty lot could be turned into a community garden at a cost less than Eden's group had originally estimated. With proximity to schools, shopping centers, and bus lines, it was a natural. The warehouse, neglected then abandoned over a period of years, would require a total overhaul to be turned into a shelter and pantry, but he estimated the cost to be less than that of building a new structure.

Now all he had to do was convince the rest of the council that the project made sense—dollars and cents, that is.

He knew how their minds worked. If a project couldn't meet the demands of their bottom line, they weren't interested. He didn't blame them. They were responsible for taxpayer dollars.

He'd scored one victory since he'd been serving on the council. After marshalling his facts and figures, he'd convinced the others to allocate more funds for the existing food pantry. Its problems were a long way from being solved, but at least now there'd be regular deliveries of food.

A dozen times, he'd picked up the phone, intending to call Eden. But something stopped him. Pride? He was honest enough to admit he suffered from an excess of it. She hadn't trusted him enough, and that had hurt.

But he'd learned something in the last couple of weeks. Pride was a lonely companion. He loved Eden, and he knew she loved him. Only one problem remained: convincing her of it.

He needed to hold her—and to be held.

She wanted nothing to do with him. She'd made that more than clear. To heck with what she wanted. He'd played by her rules; now it was time he started making some of his own.

"A what?" Harry Roberts demanded the following day as Adam outlined his plans for turning the empty lot into a community garden and a store from which participants could sell their excess produce. The warehouse would be converted into a new shelter and a community food pantry as well.

"Shut up, Harry," one of the other council members said good-naturedly. "Let Adam have his say."

Adam shot a smile at the woman, then lowered a hip onto the conference table. "I factored what it would cost to demolish the warehouse compared with what it would cost to convert it into a community building. We'll spend more money originally, but we'll recoup it and at the same time provide jobs for over one hundred unemployed men and women. That's in addition to providing food for people, for *children*," he stressed, "who are now going hungry."

Adam spent the next hour convincing the other members of the council that his plan made sense. He handed out a list of figures showing how much the county spent every year on medical care for children who lacked proper nutrition. "We'll save money *and* lives. We help others and come out looking good at the same time." He'd added the last as a further incentive.

"Sounds like it could work," Harry said cautiously at the end of Adam's presentation. "Good job."

"Thanks," Adam said, trying to hide his elation. He made the appropriate noises as the other council members filed past, but his mind was elsewhere.

Tomorrow was Christmas. Eden didn't know it yet, but he planned on spending it with her.

And the grayness that had colored his days finally lifted.

Christmas Day, Eden looked around the shelter's kitchen in satisfaction. The spicy scent of sausage competed with the equally spicy scent of frioles. Black-eyed peas sat alongside latkes. A traditional clove-studded ham took center stage.

"Doc Hathaway, you there?" a voice called from the dining hall.

Eden pushed through the swinging doors of the kitchen and saw Hattie and Norman.

"We've come to help," Hattie announced.

"That's right." Norman hefted two boxes. "We thought you might need a couple extra pair of hands."

"Just show us what needs doing." Hattie was already wheeling herself down the narrow aisles between the tables.

"You're both wonderful, but you ought to be home enjoying the holiday."

Hattie fixed her with a stern look. "Christmas is about rejoicing, not sitting on your duff watching life when we could be living it. Norman and I have a lot to be grateful for this year." She reached for her husband's hand and, finding it, brought it to her cheek.

For a moment, only a moment, Eden allowed herself to remember a time when she'd done the same with Adam, and sadness tucked itself into her heart. Pain held on, because to let go was to accept the loss.

She shook away the memory. She refused to dwell on the ragged pieces of her broken heart, especially on this most special of days,

"We still have to set the tables, carve the ham, and pour the punch."

"Norman's a world-class carver," Hattie said. "And if you'll give me the dishes and silverware, I'll set the tables." Without missing a beat, she added, "Adam stopped by a couple of days ago."

Eden busied herself rearranging a centerpiece that needed no attention. "Oh?"

Hattie eyed her shrewdly. "Seemed awful lonely. Said you and he had stopped seeing each other."

Eden felt a twist of yearning curl around her heart, and she closed her eyes against the pain. She tried to close her thoughts and heart as well, with little success. She picked up a napkin and shredded it in her fingers. "We really weren't right for each other."

"Hogwash. That boy loves you. Any fool can see it."

"We're too different from each other."

"That's good."

"Good?"

Hattie nodded emphatically. "Being different is always good. It's being too much alike that causes problems. Take Norman and me. He's on the quiet side, and I'm apt to be a mite talkative." She paused, inviting Eden to share a smile with her. "Wouldn't do at all if we both wanted to talk all the time or we were both quiet as church mice."

"No, I guess it wouldn't," Eden murmured.

"See?" Hattie demanded triumphantly. "Different is good. So what's the problem between you and Adam?"

Eden sighed, knowing Hattie Zwiebel wouldn't budge until she had an answer. "Adam voted against the site for the community garden. Even knowing what it meant to me, he voted against it."

"Did he say why?"

"He said something about its not being the best location, which I already knew. But we were desperate." She folded her arms over her chest in a defensive gesture.

"Still, maybe Adam was right."

Eden felt as if she'd been kicked in the gut. That was the second time she'd heard this from a close friend. She'd expected Hattie, of all people, to understand how she felt and to back her up.

"How can you say that?"

"Because I know you." Hattie speared her with an unflinching gaze. "When you believe in something, you go full speed ahead. Right?"

Eden nodded reluctantly. "Anything wrong with that?"

"No. If it doesn't blind you to the facts." Hattie patted Eden's hand. "You'd be the best one to decide that."

Eden was still reeling under Hattie's gentle censure when the old woman startled her once more.

"You have a lot of love to give—to me, Norman, your patients. Don't you think it's time you shared some of it with Adam? That man loves you, honey."

"How do you find your way back?" Eden wondered aloud. "How do you find the way when what's most important crumbles beneath you?"

Hattie raised calm and knowing eyes to gaze straight into Eden's. "You love each other. That's where you start, and where, if you work hard enough and long enough, you end. The young sometimes think the hardest thing in the world is finding someone to love you. When you're a bit older, you learn that the hardest thing is finding the courage to love him back."

Eden barely had a moment to think about that when Hattie asked, "What does Adam do when he believes in something?"

"He goes after it and—" Eden stopped, frowning.

Hadn't she been attracted to Adam in the first place because he fought for what he believed?

She'd been so sure she was right about the garden site. But, a niggling voice asked, hadn't Adam been equally sure he was right? Had she asked him to choose between what *he* believed and her?

"He fights for what he thinks is right," she said at last.

Hattie smiled. "Maybe you two have more in common than you thought."

Eden's hand trembled, and the juice she was pouring spilled onto the paper tablecloth.

"Not to fuss," Hattie said, blotting up the liquid with a napkin.

Eden looked up to find both Hattie and Norman looking at her, love shining from their eyes. Eden tried to keep her mind on what she was doing, but her thoughts kept returning to Adam. She was setting out foam plates when she saw him.

Dressed in chinos and a navy sweater, he looked more handsome than ever. He also looked a bit unsure of himself.

Her stomach jittered, but it wasn't nerves she felt. It was, she realized in wonder, a kind of joy.

She tried to frown, to work up some righteous indignation. Self-preservation. That's what it was. If she could hide behind anger, she wouldn't have to face the truth.

"What are you doing here?" she asked, then flushed at her less than gracious tone. She tried to keep her heart cold and still but realized she had failed miserably when it gave a leap of happiness.

"Making things right, I hope."

She looked at him, really looked at him, and saw the fine lines etched along his brow and bracketing his mouth. The last couple of weeks hadn't been easy for him either, she realized.

Adam took the items from her and finished setting out the plates.

Then he rolled up his sleeves. "Tell me what else needs to be done."

"You . . . uh . . . could help Hattie and Norman serve."

Eden was acutely aware of Hattie and Norman's approving looks as Adam joined them behind the huge serving table. She thought she saw Norman give Adam a thumbs-up sign but decided she must've been mistaken.

Richard pronounced the blessing on the food and invited everyone to get in line. Eden and Richard kept the bowls and platters filled while Adam, Norman, and Hattie dished out the food.

Eden glanced up at one time to find Adam watching her. Flustered, she stabbed her fingers through her hair to push it back from her forehead, aware how hot and disheveled she must look.

Finally, everyone had been served.

Eden sank down on a chair and sighed. "I don't know about the rest of you, but I'm starved. What do you say we fill our plates and—"

"Sorry," Hattie interrupted. "Norman and I've got to go."

Eden watched as Hattie and Norman exchanged guilty looks. "Can't you stay for a little while longer?"

But Norman was already pushing Hattie's wheelchair down an aisle between tables and waving over his shoulder. "See you," he called. "Merry Christmas!"

"Oh, well." Eden turned to Richard Nolan and the other servers. "The rest of us can still enjoy dinner. I think there's even some of Hattie's pie left."

Richard checked his watch. "I've got to go too." He looked around, anywhere but at her. "Don't worry about cleaning up. I've got some volunteers coming in to do that. Have a merry Christmas, Eden."

She felt her self-assurance slipping as she was left alone with Adam. "I'll just fix us some plates, and we can—"

He took her hand. "We've got some talking to do first."

"But what about dinner?"

"We'll find something along the way." He picked up her coat and draped it over her shoulders.

"On the way? On the way where?" she asked as she pushed her arms through the sleeves.

"You'll see."

"What are we going to find open on Christmas Day?" She was tired, hungry, and feeling out of sorts. Norman, Hattie, and even Richard had taken off with scarcely a good-bye.

She'd planned on having Christmas dinner with them. Also, she admitted to herself, she'd needed them around to act as a buffer between herself and Adam.

"I don't want a hamburger on Christmas," she said, sounding petulant. "I want ham and sweet potatoes and pumpkin pie."

Adam hustled her out the back door and bundled her into his car. He turned on the heater as she fastened her seat belt.

His shoulder brushed hers as he shifted into gear. She found his quiet strength as appealing as ever. She loved this man. Whatever he'd done, whatever his reasons, she loved him. She couldn't—wouldn't—deny it any longer.

A faint smile wisped around his mouth. "We might be able to arrange that."

"I don't want to have Christmas dinner in a restaurant," she said, knowing she sounded cross but not caring. "I want to have it with my friends."

"You know what? You sure complain a lot." He made a point of taking her hand and entwining their fingers, which made her feel a little better, if thoroughly confused. "Now, be quiet before I forget that I love you," he ordered.

"You love me?"

"I'll always love you. Don't you know that?"

She tried not to soften when his hand squeezed hers. His touch was nearly unbearable in its tenderness.

She couldn't help it. She went warm and gooey all over, like a chocolate bar left too long in the sun. It was the way he'd said it, the way he looked at her, that had her pulse thumping under her skin.

Adam stopped the car and leaned across the seat. She tried to evade him, knowing she'd be lost if he kissed her. But he held her fast. And his kiss, as gentle as a summer breeze, broke down her defenses until she relaxed in his arms.

He ended the kiss. "I should've done this two weeks ago."

She buried her face against his throat before forcing herself to meet his gaze. "It doesn't change anything," she said, her voice hitching.

His chuckle was soft and stirring. "If you don't be quiet, I'll have to do it again."

"But—"

"See what I mean? Some people just don't learn the first time." He kissed her again.

This time she didn't protest. It had been too long. She curled her arms around his neck, no longer caring what had gone before.

"Why? Why did you come?" she asked after he broke the kiss. Her breath shortened, thickened. "I can't bear to send you away again."

"It's going to be all right, sweetheart."

Eden sank back into the seat, unable to fight him any longer. Whatever he'd done, she loved him. She watched as he restarted the car and maneuvered through traffic to arrive at the lot next to the abandoned warehouse, where weeds and piles of trash grew with equal enthusiasm.

"If this is some kind of joke—"

"The city doesn't like empty lots," he said conversationally as he parked. "In fact, they're considered a real blight, a hazard. An insurance nightmare."

"What does that have to do with anything?"

"Did you know there are two elementary schools in this district? A bus line runs straight through here. There's also a shopping center within walking distance. There're water lines available. The city's offering incentives to develop the property. Into a new shelter and a community garden."

"The garden? Oh, Adam, it's perfect! Absolutely perfect! How long have you known about it?"

"A day or so."

"Why didn't you tell me?"

"I wanted to make absolutely sure before I told you. I didn't want you to be disappointed again."

"I'm sorry about what I said," she said, her voice no more than a husky whisper. "You didn't deserve that."

"You were hurting."

"That doesn't excuse what I said. I should've known better. I *did* know better." The first hint of a watery smile moved over her lips.

He traced the curve of her cheek, then replaced his finger with his lips.

"Now that we've got that settled, I've got a proposition for you."

"Just what kind of proposition?" She cocked her head to one side. "One always has to be very careful what kind of proposition one accepts."

"It's a pretty serious one. Are you willing to take on a man who tends to be stubborn, opinionated, and likes his own way?"

"It depends."

"On what?"

"On whether he's willing to take on a woman who's equally stubborn, opinionated, and likes her own way."

"Oh, he's willing, all right. Is there any hope these two stubborn, opinionated, strong-willed people can get together?"

"All the hope in the world." Eden punctuated her pronouncement by kissing him. She smiled at him with a warmth that felt like a benediction.

"What about it? Are you willing to take on a hardheaded ex-cop turned politician?"

"If you can handle a busy-as-blazes doctor."

"I can. And I promise to love you for the rest of my life."

"That's a proposition I can accept and match."

Chapter Twelve

Adam helped Eden over the pitted and littered ground flanking the abandoned warehouse.

"Shouldn't that be locked?" she asked when he pushed open the warehouse door.

"Probably," he agreed, but he didn't sound overly concerned.

"Someone's here," she whispered, hearing footsteps above them. She clutched Adam's arm. "Maybe we should call the police."

"Let's take a look first. We don't want to call the cops on a false alarm." Adam pushed the button of a freight elevator and took her hand.

"This place has electricity?" Eden asked.

"Apparently. Watch your step."

Adam pulled open the grilled door of the elevator and pushed the button for the second floor. Eden held her breath as the car groaned to a start and then wheezed its way up.

She tugged at his hand. "I hear something." Even above the noise of the elevator, some kind of racket was audible.

"Then we'd better investigate."

"I love you already," she said, caught between rampant curiosity and alarm. "You don't have to play hero for me."

He kissed her nose. "I love you too."

"That's not the point," she said impatiently. "We don't know what we'll find up there."

The elevator grumbled to a stop.

"I thought you liked surprises." The door opened, and he pulled her inside.

"Merry Christmas!" The shouted greeting from a dozen or more voices caused her to stop and stare at a long table elegantly set with plates and cutlery.

But it wasn't the table that drew her attention or the savory aromas coming from the steaming covered dishes upon it. It was the people.

She took an inventory of the smiling faces.

Zach and Anna Connelly, along with Teddy. Mrs. Longstreet and the rest of the hospital auxiliary league, plus Mr. Cheston. Richard from the shelter. Cuddlers, parents, and nurses from the preemie unit at the hospital. In the back were Norman and Hattie. And Adam's parents.

"How did . . . what are . . ." She forced back the tears that threatened to spill over as she kissed each of the people who had become so dear to her.

"We had to break every speed rule in the book to beat you and Adam here," Richard said after giving her a quick hug.

"That's right," Norman seconded, pushing Hattie's wheel-chair closer to Eden. "Richard nearly scared us to death with his driving. But we made it."

Adam came to stand behind her, wrapping his arms around her waist.

Eden would have reached for Hattie if she hadn't been loving the feel of Adam's arms around her so much. There was something new in his embrace, something infinitely sweet, something . . . permanent.

The world was filled with promise and hope and love. Eden scrubbed the heels of her hands over damp eyes.

"We thought you'd catch on for sure," Hattie said. "The look on your face when we said we had to leave . . . you about had me in tears. I almost spilled the surprise then and there."

"You made us feel right bad," Norman agreed. "But we knew you'd forgive us when you saw Adam's surprise."

"You knew about this? All of you?"

Hattie chuckled. "Sure did. Adam told us. Said he needed our help to give you the best Christmas ever."

"We fixed a real old-fashioned Christmas dinner," Mrs. Longstreet said, hugging Eden and pecking Adam on the cheek. "We'd best be sitting down and eating before everything gets cold. Nothing worse than cold mashed potatoes."

The tears would no longer be denied, and Eden's eyes filled as she looked at her friends—*family,* she corrected herself—crowded around her.

"I love you," Adam said quietly, easing her around in his arms to kiss her. "Merry Christmas."

Her heart turned over. She knew Adam's love for her was sure and true and that he loved her as much as she did him. The feelings she had at this moment would stay in her memory, and her heart, forever.

She gave herself up to the sweeping tenderness his kisses always produced. "And I love you. For always."